DUMB LUCK

"He's cheating me out of my money. I can't afford to lose all this money."

"Weeell," Nate whined, "then you shouldn't have gambled it."

Clint let out an aggravated breath, wondering how the hell someone could have been stupid enough to say those words at that particular time. The moment alone convinced him Nate was no cheater. No cheater in his right mind would have prodded someone like that after taking a pot.

"Come on now," Clint said quickly. "This doesn't have to get ugly."

But the young man was already past listening to what anyone had to say. His eyes were fixed on Nate, his jaw was clenched, and his hand was gripping the side of the table.

At that moment, Clint felt a stab of panic in his gut. Only one of the young man's hands was on the table. The other was down at his side, already wrapped around his gun. Before Clint could do a thing about it, the young man pulled his trigger and sent a round up through the table . . .

THE GUNSMITH

290

THE GRAND PRIZE

J. R. ROBERTS

J

JOVE BOOKS, NEW YORK

THE BERKLEY PUBLISHING GROUP
Published by the Penguin Group
Penguin Group (USA) Inc.
375 Hudson Street, New York, New York 10014, USA
Penguin Group (Canada), 90 Eglinton Avenue East, Suite 700, Toronto, Ontario M4P 2Y3, Canada
(a division of Pearson Penguin Canada Inc.)
Penguin Books Ltd., 80 Strand, London WC2R 0RL, England
Penguin Group Ireland, 25 St. Stephen's Green, Dublin 2, Ireland (a division of Penguin Books Ltd.)
Penguin Group (Australia), 250 Camberwell Road, Camberwell, Victoria 3124, Australia
(a division of Pearson Australia Group Pty. Ltd.)
Penguin Books India Pvt. Ltd., 11 Community Centre, Panchsheel Park, New Delhi—110 017, India
Penguin Group (NZ), Cnr. Airborne and Rosedale Roads, Albany, Auckland 1310, New Zealand
(a division of Pearson New Zealand Ltd.)
Penguin Books (South Africa) (Pty.) Ltd., 24 Sturdee Avenue, Rosebank, Johannesburg 2196,
South Africa

Penguin Books Ltd., Registered Offices: 80 Strand, London WC2R 0RL, England

This is a work of fiction. Names, characters, places, and incidents either are the product of the author's imagination or are used fictitiously, and any resemblance to actual persons, living or dead, business establishments, events, or locales is entirely coincidental.

THE GRAND PRIZE

A Jove Book / published by arrangement with the author

PRINTING HISTORY
Jove edition / February 2006

Copyright © 2006 by Robert J. Randisi.

ISBN: 0-515-14070-8

JOVE®
Jove Books are published by The Berkley Publishing Group,
a division of Penguin Group (USA) Inc.,
375 Hudson Street, New York, New York 10014.
JOVE is a registered trademark of Penguin Group (USA) Inc.
The "J" design is a trademark belonging to Penguin Group (USA) Inc.

PRINTED IN THE UNITED STATES OF AMERICA

10 9 8 7 6 5 4 3 2 1

ONE

Nate DeLouse was a lucky man.

Clint had seen it plenty of times. Even though many card-players insisted that they relied only on skill, all of those men were either trying to impress someone or fooling themselves. There was some skill involved, but luck was the bullet in the chamber. Without a bullet to fire, it didn't make much difference how quick a man was on the draw.

Nate's smirk was more of a twitch. It looked even more awkward because he was trying so desperately to cover it up. Finally, he just reached up and pretended to scratch a spot just beneath his nose.

"I raise," Nate said.

There were two other men left at the table besides Clint. One of them was a kid who only played when he was certain he could win, and the other was a middle-aged man in a rumpled suit who'd obviously played a few hands in his time.

The man in the suit glanced over to Clint and winked. "What do you say, Adams? Should I call or do you think he's bluffing again?"

Clint shrugged and shot a glance over to Nate. The scrawny fellow was still scratching at his upper lip.

"I don't know," Clint mused. "But if that scratch isn't a tell, then he's got a tick burrowing into his mustache."

The other three laughed at Clint's comment, but Nate's was more of a forced series of coughs that seemed even more awkward than his persistent scratching.

Nate DeLouse squirmed in his seat, but that didn't tell anyone much of anything. Not only had he been squirming throughout the whole game, but he seemed to be uncomfortable in his own skin. The clothes he wore added yet another level to his discomfort. Whenever Nate squirmed or shifted one way, his clothes seemed to go the other way until they managed to twist themselves around him like he was being wrung out.

His face was narrow and lumpy, marked by close-set eyes, a long nose, and a set of oddly spaced teeth that seemed to be just a little too big for his mouth. When he spoke, his words always started out as a whine before finally gaining enough steam to form syllables.

"Ehhh, I guess you'll all just have to see for yourselves," Nate said, making a conscious effort to leave his lip alone.

Clint leaned back in his chair and fixed Nate with a stare. "See what?"

There was no threat in Clint's eyes, but there seemed to be something in there to make Nate nervous. "S-s-see if I got anything worth betting on."

"Oh, yeah. That."

All this time, the man in the suit had been watching the two men. His eyes came to rest on Nate and stayed there. When he caught Nate looking at him quickly before turning away twice as fast, the man smiled confidently. "I call," he said as he shoved some money into the middle of the table.

Nate's smile grew, but his head turned as though someone had raised a hand to him. "What about you, Clint?"

Clint hadn't taken his eyes off Nate yet. As with any

other game, he'd been watching the other players to see how they reacted, what hands they carried through to the end, and how they acted before laying their cards down.

In the space of half an hour, Clint thought he had a pretty good read on all of the men at the table. For Nate, however, he needed one more hand to be sure.

"All right, Nate," Clint said with a resigned sigh. "Let's see what you got."

The youngest man at the table had been darting his eyes back and forth between Clint and Nate. When he saw Clint shove his money into the middle, his eyes lingered on the sizable stack of cash. After studying his cards some more, he nodded and announced, "I'm in, too."

Clint was holding a pair of fours with a queen to go along for the ride. If he was in this to win a single pot, he would have laid down that little pair without hesitation. But Clint never played a game for a single pot. Like anything else, a card game had a big picture and that was what he wanted to see.

"All right, Nate," the man in the suit said. "You've been called. Let's see what you've got."

Nate's head twitched to the side and his smile flickered across his face. He repeated that series of movements a few more times until Clint started to think that Nate might be having a nervous fit.

Finally, Nate laid down his cards to reveal the jack of clubs at the front, with four more clubs right behind it. "Ehh, looks like a flush to me."

"Beats my three kings," the man in the suit declared. "And I thought I had you, too."

Clint dropped his fours and winced. The expression wasn't too convincing, but he wasn't exactly playing to an expert crowd, either. "I thought you were bluffing. Guess that'll teach me."

The younger man wasn't so cavalier about it. Still gripping his cards, he looked back and forth between his hand

and Nate's. Every time he looked back, his eyes darted faster and faster between the two hands.

"Can you beat it or not?" the man in the suit asked. "If it takes this long for you to figure it out, you shouldn't be playing for money."

Clint watched the young man carefully. There was something in his eyes that didn't set right. It was a fiery glint that grew hotter every time he looked back and forth between his hand and Nate's.

"If you got beat, you don't need to show," Clint offered. "Just lay them down and we can play the next hand."

Now, the young man started shaking his head. "He cheated," he whispered. "He had to have cheated."

Nate twitched and started mimicking the young man's eye movements. Only, he wasn't looking at the cards but was more interested in the gun hands of the players.

"N-n-now that's not true," Nate stammered while nervously patting the table. "Let's not start throwing those kind of words around."

The young man's eyes stopped darting and settled on Nate's face. From there, they slowly started to narrow into angry slits. "He cheated. You can see it on his face."

Clint leaned forward so he could put himself into the young man's line of sight. "Can you prove that?"

"I don't have to. I know it for a fact. He's cheating me out of my money. I can't afford to lose all this money."

"Weeell," Nate whined, "then you shouldn't have gambled it."

Clint let out an aggravated breath, wondering how the hell someone could have been stupid enough to say those words at that particular time. That moment alone convinced him that Nate was no cheater. No cheater in his right mind would have prodded someone like that after taking a pot.

"Come on now," Clint said quickly. "This doesn't have to get ugly."

But the young man was already past listening to what anyone had to say. His eyes were fixed on Nate, his jaw was clenched, and his hand was gripping the side of the table.

At that moment, Clint felt a stab of panic in his gut. Only one of the young man's hands was on the table. The other was down at his side, already wrapped around his gun. Before Clint could do a thing about it, the young man pulled his trigger and sent a round up through the table to hiss past Nate's chin.

At that moment, Nate DeLouse was the luckiest man in West Texas.

TWO

Nate was still reeling back from the shot that had just come from under the table. His first instinct was to push himself back as quick as he could, even though he was nowhere near quick enough to dodge a bullet. He had the thickness of the table itself to thank since that's what diverted the bullet from hitting him in the face.

As it was, Nate felt the lead whip past him so close that it clipped a few whiskers of his mustache as it went by. His eyes widened and his jaw hung open. His arms also started flapping on either side of him, but that seemed more because he was teetering on the back two legs of his chair.

The young man was pushing himself away from the table and bringing his gun up so he could take another shot. Although his eyes were fixed intently on Nate, he had the expression of someone who wasn't sure if he was really doing what he was doing or simply dreaming it.

Clint, however, knew exactly what he was doing. Rather than draw the modified Colt from its holster, he lunged to his side and twisted from his chair with both arms extended toward the younger man. His left arm connected first, brushing against the other's shirt and skidding over his chest.

6

Clint's right arm stretched out so he could grab hold of the young man's gun hand at the wrist. The moment his fingers closed around that wrist, Clint pushed the young man back while forcing his aim up toward the ceiling.

As the young man fell back, his arm went up. Another round exploded from his barrel and went right where Clint was hoping. The bullet took a chunk from one of the rafters and sent a flutter of dust and wood down onto the neighboring table.

Although he'd been caught off his guard at first, the young man came around quickly once he felt himself falling backward to the floor. He was still angry, and only got angrier when he saw that he was being taken down.

"Let go of the gun, kid," Clint said after rolling off the edge of the table to accompany the young man to the floor. "You don't want to do this."

But Clint knew what the response would be even before the first word came from the young man's mouth. The expression on his face said it all: He'd gone this far and figured it was too late to turn back now.

"You let go of me!" the young man spat back. "Are you in on this with him? Are you a cheater, too?"

"I'm just trying to keep you from making a real big mistake. Let go of the gun. Now!"

With an effort that took Clint by surprise, the young man pulled his gun hand free and twisted around, away from him. That put him on his belly on the floor, while also keeping the gun in his possession.

Having landed on his side, Clint could feel the stab of pain in his ribs. He climbed to his feet and knew by the time he was up that he'd merely bruised his side without breaking anything. Now that he was on his feet, he could move around and over the young man. He could also get a better look at what was going on around him.

The saloon where their game was being played was a big place, but was drafty as a barn. Half of the room was cluttered with old tables and broken chairs, while the other half was filled with a few occupied tables and a sorry excuse for a bar.

A few men leaned against the crates and boards that passed for a bar and the rest were seated around the three occupied card tables. One of those tables had cleared out at the first sign of trouble, while the men at the other were leaning back and watching the fight as if it was a show.

What interested Clint more was what was happening at his own table. At one end, right where Clint had left him, Nate was still wobbling back and forth on his teetering chair while flapping his arms like a lanky bird.

Clint almost couldn't get himself to look away from the odd sight of Nate trying to keep his balance. Suddenly, at the bottom of his field of vision, he saw the young man on the floor getting up and lifting his gun one more time.

Since he couldn't reach the kid's gun at that second, Clint did the next best thing and reached out for the one thing he could. Leaning out and stretching his arm until his shoulder hurt, Clint tapped Nate on the chest and sent him flapping all the way to the floor.

Nate hit with a jarring thud that could be felt right up through the floorboards.

The young man's gun went off, sending a round through the air where Nate had previously been.

Clint was now able to step forward and grab hold of the young man's wrist. "Sorry, kid," he said just as his fist was snapping down to crack against the young man's jaw.

It wasn't a hard punch, but the downward angle gave it an extra kick. Clint's knuckles glanced off the young man's face and rattled his head back and forth. The young man let go of his gun reflexively, allowing Clint to take it away from him without any more fuss.

Flipping the gun from one hand to another, Clint stuffed it under his belt and looked down at the kid, who was still curled up on the floor. Nudging him with the toe of his boot, Clint asked, "You got any more guns, kid?"

Still rubbing his jaw, the young man shook his head.

Clint looked around and saw that he was the center of attention. When he found the man who was running the place, he pointed to the kid on the floor and said, "Better take this one somewhere he can cool off."

The man who'd been serving drinks wiped his hands on the apron around his waist and waddled from behind the bar. "You want me to call the sheriff?"

"I don't know," Clint replied as he walked around the table to where Nate was flopping on the floor. "Why not ask *him*?"

Clint offered a hand to Nate, who grabbed hold of it in a clammy grip. When he was hoisted to his feet, his body felt more like a limp fish flailing at the wrong end of a hook.

"Nnnah," Nate said.

For a moment, Clint couldn't decide if that was Nate's answer or just a noise he was making while getting pulled to his feet.

Nate shook his head as his awkward smirk reappeared on his face. "Guess we don't have to bother. Buuut I think it's a good idea to keep his gun away from—"

"Say no more," Clint said. With a snap of a wrist, he plucked the gun from his belt and tossed it toward the bartender.

Although he caught the pistol, the bartender didn't look like he knew what to do with it.

Clint looked down at the kid and extended an open hand. "Come on. Up and at 'em."

When he saw Clint's hand, the kid reflexively twitched. He then grimaced at his own reaction and instead took hold of the help he was being offered. Compared to Nate, he made it back to his feet with the grace of a dancer.

"What now?" the kid asked tentatively.

Clint righted his chair and sat down in it. The man in the suit beside him hadn't even moved from his spot.

"I suggest you step outside and get some fresh air," Clint said. "After that, the day's pretty much yours."

Gathering up the cards that had been spilled across the table, Clint shuffled them and looked at the other two remaining players.

"Ante up."

THREE

Clint stepped out of the drafty place where he'd been playing cards and stretched his arms over his head. It had been
a long day, which had turned into an even longer night. After taking a few steps outside, he turned on the balls of his
feet and took a look at the saloon.

It was one of those places that seemed bigger on the inside than it did on the outside. From where he was standing, the place looked like any number of two-floor houses
that had been gutted and turned into something else. Inside, without anything above the main floor other than a set
of dusty rafters, the place seemed better suited for horses
than people.

Shaking his head, Clint put the place behind him and
walked down the street. The town was called Carte Nueves
and was situated in an otherwise barren stretch of West
Texas land not too far from Labyrinth. It was a fair-sized
town with enough residents to fill the streets during the
day. Other than that, Clint didn't really know that much
about it.

When he'd left the saloon, Clint's intention had been to
buckle Eclipse into his saddle and head back to Labyrinth.
Now, after a few deep breaths of the nighttime air, Clint

didn't even have the gumption to lift his arms any longer. A saddle seemed like a pipe dream.

The sky stretched out over his head the way it only seemed to in Texas. It was a sea of black filled with more twinkling gems than he could possibly imagine. Looking up at it for a few seconds, Clint felt like he might start teetering backward like Nate DeLouse in his chair.

"You sure you didn't cheat?" came a voice from the direction of the saloon.

"Weeell, that's not my way of doing things."

Clint rolled his eyes and cursed himself for not getting out of town when he'd had the chance.

The saloon's door had been ajar already, and was now pushed open by the two remaining players from Clint's card game. Oddly enough, the man in the suit had taken a shine to Nate DeLouse over the course of the last half of their game. The two of them sure made an odd couple as Nate seemed engulfed by the arm that was draped over his shoulder.

"There you are, Adams!" the man in the suit declared. "I must say, that was one hell of a game. Yes, sir, one hell of a game."

"I managed to break even," Clint said.

"I don't mind telling you that I'd gladly hand over my own winnings if I could see that brawl one more time."

"Sorry," Clint replied with a shrug. "I don't take requests."

The man's face practically split apart in a smile, but he didn't make a sound. Instead, the laugh he wanted to get out seemed to be caught in the back of his throat. Either that, or it had died from all the whiskey the man had been knocking back.

"No requests?" the man finally sputtered. "That's funny!"

Clint nodded and started walking down the street. "Yeah, well, it's been a pleasure."

"Where are you going? I hear there's a hell of a game

going on at another place down the road. Why don't you join us and we'll see what kind of hell we can raise?"

"You go on without me. I'm tired."

"Yeah," Nate said as he squirmed out from under the man's arm. "You go on ahead and, ehhhh, I'll meet you there."

"I'll see the both of you at that game," the man said as he struggled to maintain his balance. "Or I'll come looking for you." With that, he tossed a flopping wave at Clint and Nate before staggering toward the next saloon he could find.

Nate spent a few moments catching up to Clint. The next few moments after that were spent trying to adjust his shirt collar and jacket back to the way they were before his newest friend had gotten ahold of them. Even after he made one last adjustment, Nate's clothes somehow managed to look more rumpled than before.

Clint knew Nate was following him. Considering the man's awkward walk and raspy breathing, there was no way for Nate to sneak up on much of anyone. Clint's biggest hope, however, was that if he ignored Nate for long enough he would just go away.

Unfortunately, Clint's luck wasn't quite so good that night.

"Hey there, Clint."

Clint kept walking, giving his hope one last set of legs before abandoning it altogether.

Before too long, Clint felt a tapping on his shoulder that was something akin to fat drops of water dripping onto his arm. He stopped, forced an amiable look onto his face, and said, "What is it, Nate?"

Nate nodded and looked around as if he'd just run into Clint by coincidence. Possibly sensing the other man's aggravation, Nate spit out what he was trying to say. "What you did back in that saloon, you think you, ehhhh, ever might want to try doing that for a living?"

That question struck Clint as odd, especially under the circumstances. "I barely broke even, Nate. That doesn't really qualify me to be a professional. Maybe you should try your hand at it."

Nate shook his head and started to laugh. His uncomfortable smile was strange-looking enough, but when he tried to laugh as well, it seemed though he was choking on a hair ball. "I don't think I'd last too long in that profession. I just got lucky tonight."

"Yeah," Clint replied. "I'd say you did. I hope you at least learned to watch what you say after you take enough of someone else's money."

"I sure have. Actually," Nate added, while removing a folded bunch of dollar bills, "I think I owe you some of this."

"No reason for that."

"Oh, I won't hear any of that."

"Seriously, keep your money."

But Nate kept pushing the cash toward Clint as if he meant to stick it straight onto his shirt.

After Clint had been smacked a few times by Nate's limp fingers and the sweaty money, he was about ready to slap the bills into the street. He realized that was the long day affecting him as much as Nate himself, so Clint took a deep breath and put a little more of an edge into his voice.

"Keep it," Clint said with finality. "I insist."

The smile was frozen on Nate's face, but that wasn't anything new. Just when it seemed he might have dozed off with his eyes open, he finally shrugged and pulled his hand back. "Aaaall right. But I'll buy the drinks next time."

"You got it," Clint said, already moving down the street at a quicker pace.

"But that offer I made, it could benefit you quite a bit."

"Don't want to be a professional gambler, Nate. Good night."

"I didn't mean gambling."

Clint stopped for a moment and thought back to what else Nate might have intended. He pondered that for all of two seconds before he realized that he didn't much care for anything else the other man had to say.

"I'm tired, Nate. We can talk about it some other time, okay?"

Even though he wasn't looking at him directly, Clint could hear the sloppy grin in Nate's voice.

"Sure thing, Clint. I'll look forward to it. Next time it is!"

Now that Clint seemed to have finally ended this conversation with Nate, he vowed to make sure there wouldn't be a next time.

FOUR

Clint was staying in a boardinghouse one street down from where he'd been playing cards. After what it had taken to get away from Nate, Clint felt as if he'd crawled through a desert just to get back into his rented room. Once he was there, however, it seemed like a major victory.

The room was small, yet comfortable. The boardinghouse was fairly empty since there weren't many other travelers in town at the moment. Those that were there stayed at the hotel, which was not only marked with a larger sign, but was also a whole lot closer to the saloons.

Seeing the small bed with the soft mattress in between the little chair and varnished dresser, Clint thought he'd sliced off a little bit of heaven. The place was quiet, fresh air spilled in through the open window, and there wasn't a trace of Nate DeLouse.

Clint eased himself down onto the edge of the bed, letting out a grateful sigh as he went. Just as his backside had settled fully into the mattress, there was the rattle of knuckles against his door.

Clint closed his eyes, as though that might help whoever was gently knocking to think he wasn't there.

After a moment of silence, the rapping continued.

16

"If that's you, Nate, I'm going to be very upset."

There was a pause and then a muffled voice from the hall said, "I'm not Kate."

Aggravated, tired, and cursing himself that he'd ever gone to Carte Nueves in the first place, Clint got up and pulled the door open.

"I didn't say Kate," he growled. "I said N   "

He stopped short when he got a look at who was standing outside his door. She was tall for a woman and fairly close to his own height. She was wearing a dress made from a loosely crocheted, light tan cotton, and a generous amount of her richly tanned skin could be seen through the weave. There wasn't enough to be considered indecent, but it was plenty to get Clint's imagination up and running.

She had dark blond hair and full, red lips. Her head was cast just downward enough so that her light blue eyes were gazing up at him in a slightly pouting manner.

"I'm sorry," the blonde said. "I don't know who Kate is, but if you want me to leave—"

Realizing that he was staring at her, Clint shook himself out of his stupor and laughed. "I should be the one apologizing," he said. "That wasn't a nice way to greet someone at the door. Although, I think you might have the wrong room."

"Are you Clint Adams?"

"I sure am."

"Then I've got the right room."

Suddenly, Clint realized where all his luck had gone. "Well, then, why not come on inside?"

She walked in a way that made the few steps from the hall and through the door seem like a parade. Her hips twitched slowly beneath her skirt and the smell of her skin brushed past him like a silky veil. After moving far enough inside for him to close the door, she stopped and turned around.

"Is Kate your wife?" she asked.

Clint shook his head. "No. I said Nate and he's not someone I want to think about right now."

Suddenly, the blonde smiled and nodded. "Oh, you mean Nate the Louse?"

The title she'd given Nate didn't exactly rhyme with his last name, but it was close enough to bring a smile to Clint's face. Even if he'd never heard Nate's last name, it was hard to deny how well the blonde's title hung on the scrawny little cuss.

"Yeah," Clint said. "That's the one. And who might you be?"

Covering her mouth in embarrassment, the blonde winced and said, "How rude of me. I'm Warren's sister, Katrina."

Clint started to nod, but then stopped just as quickly. "Wait a moment. Who's Warren?"

"Warren Nolen." When she saw that Clint's confused expression still hadn't changed, she added, "The man who you kept from making a big mistake today at the card table."

That brought a reaction and Clint snapped his fingers when the young man's face popped into his mind. "The kid who took a shot at Nate."

"That's the one."

"You're his sister?"

She nodded. "Katrina Nolen."

"Pleased to meet you. Sorry if my memory is a little slow. It's been a real long day."

"Yes, I heard that you just got into town earlier this afternoon?"

"That's right. I rode out from Labyrinth just to let my horse stretch his legs and I wound up in a card game. I rented this room just to have a quiet place to sit and wash up, and then got wrapped up in the game. I guess you know how things went from there."

Katrina nodded and let out a heavy sigh. "Things did

take a bad turn, but they could have been a whole lot worse. If Warren had killed Nate, he would have been put in jail. Or . . . worse."

"After spending some time with Nate, I think that plenty of folks around here wouldn't have minded if your brother would have hit him with that shot."

"A few folks might have even given Warren a reward, but the law still frowns on gunplay like that here in town. Besides, I don't think he could have lived with that on his conscience. Even if he was only shooting at the Louse."

Katrina looked around and let her eyes linger on Clint's bed. When she looked back at him, her cheeks were blossoming with a hint of extra color. "I hope I'm not keeping you from anything."

"I was just going to say the same thing."

She shook her head. "No, I just wanted to meet you. I mean," she quickly added, "just so I could thank you for helping my brother."

There was something about the way Katrina was looking at him that struck Clint as familiar. Perhaps it was more the way she looked from a certain angle. "Hold on. Were you at the card game today?"

She smirked a bit and nodded.

"I thought I recognized you," Clint said. "It took me a moment, but you did stick in my mind."

"I was there for a little while. Normally, I like to watch my brother play. Once he started losing, though, I couldn't bear to watch. I heard about what happened after I left from a friend of mine."

Clint moved in another step closer. It was more than instinct that drew him to her. It was something in the way she cocked her head a bit and looked at him; almost as if she was beckoning him to come to her. When he got there, he noticed that she didn't make the slightest attempt to move away.

Reaching up, Clint brushed the edge of his finger underneath Katrina's chin. Her skin was smooth and soft to the touch. "You know, a lady as pretty as yourself might just have been a lucky charm for any man while she was there."

There had been a touch of shyness in her expression when she'd first stepped into Clint's room. Now, however, it was nowhere to be found. "I'm here now," she whispered. "Do you feel lucky?"

"Let's put it to the test." With that, Clint leaned in and kissed her gently upon the mouth.

Katrina let out a satisfied breath and melted into Clint's arms.

FIVE

Katrina's body had been tense when Clint first put his arms around her. Then, as their kiss became more passionate, she relaxed against him and moved her hands up and down along his back. As Clint moved his hands over her body, he could feel her becoming tense again. This time, however, that tension had nothing at all to do with nervousness.

"I was watching you in that saloon," she whispered. "I watched you and wanted to be right here the whole time."

Her hands clenched on the back of his shirt and yanked it from where it had been tucked into his pants. She moved her hands underneath the material so she could feel his skin. From there, she brushed her fingers along Clint's ribs and worked her way to his stomach.

"I thought about touching you," she breathed once their lips moved apart. "And more," she added, tugging open his pants and easing them down. Her hands slipped between Clint's legs to feel his growing erection. "So much more."

Clint felt like his senses were flooded with her. Katrina's skin and hair brushed against him. Her scent filled his nose and now the taste of her lips ran like honey in his mouth. He could hear nothing but her breathy voice and

21

could see nothing but her eyes looking at him before she started lowering herself down onto her knees.

Never letting her hands stray from him, Katrina let her fingers wander over Clint's legs and thighs after she took his belt and pants off. She then focused her attention on his rigid penis while she slowly reached up to cup him in both hands.

She looked up into his eyes as she opened her mouth and moved forward. Clint looked down at her pretty blue eyes until he felt her hot breath on him. Then, he watched her sweet red lips part and take him inside. Her tongue flicked out just before she closed her mouth, teasing the length of his cock.

Clint's hands found their way to the back of her head. His fingers threaded through her hair and he felt the instant she started bobbing her head back and forth. Although he could direct the way she moved, he quickly decided that she didn't need any guidance.

It was much better for him to let her move at her own pace. That way, he could be surprised when she suddenly sucked on him faster or slowed down to taste every inch of him as if she was savoring a stick of candy.

When her tongue began massaging him as well, Clint felt his breath start to come in quick, shallow gulps. Reluctantly, he eased her back.

"What's the matter?" she asked with a little pout, which made her look even sexier on her knees in front of him. "Did I do something wrong?"

Clint had to laugh as he helped her to her feet. "You didn't do a thing wrong. Maybe you did it a little too well."

"Really?" she asked innocently. "What do you mean?"

"Here," he replied. "Let me show you."

Clint undressed her. Katrina moved to make things easier for him, but plainly enjoyed the way he peeled the layers of clothing off her body. Once he had her completely naked, Clint guided her to the bed to lie down.

Shrugging off the rest of his own clothes, Clint climbed onto the bed and crawled on top of her. The more he rubbed against her body, the more Katrina smiled. When she felt Clint's rigid cock moving between her legs, the smile took on more of a wanton urgency.

Katrina's legs opened for him, allowing Clint to settle in between them. He could feel the wetness between her legs as he ground his hips against hers. When his cock rubbed against a certain spot, she sucked in a quick breath and arched her back slightly beneath him.

Now it was Clint's turn to smile as he slid once again down the length of her body. Katrina had a trim build with pert breasts capped with small, hard nipples. As he worked his way down, Clint flicked his tongue against her nipples, letting one of them briefly brush against his teeth.

With that little touch against her sensitive breasts, Katrina made little scratches against his shoulders as her fingers dug in with surprise. Her touch lightened immediately as she felt his lips work their way over her flat belly and down to the smoother skin just above the soft hair between her legs.

Clint started out kissing her gently. He moved down until his lips were teasing her clitoris. When he felt her touch turn into an iron grip on his shoulders, he knew he was in the right area.

Katrina's skin tasted sweet and her body trembled slightly under him. Soon, his mouth was brushing against her pussy and his tongue flicked out to slip inside her.

"Oh, my God," she breathed as her hips pressed up against Clint's face.

Before she could get too comfortable, Clint shifted his attention up a bit until he was making a little circle around her clitoris with the tip of his tongue. Before too long, she was trembling every time he tasted her and Katrina was the one to start pushing him away.

Clint wasn't able to get more than half an inch back before he felt her fingers clenching in his hair. Following her guidance, he remained between her legs with his tongue working busily in and on her wet pussy. He could feel her bucking against his face as her breaths came out in long moans.

Soon, Katrina's breath caught in her throat and she froze with her eyes wide open. Staring at the ceiling overhead, she let out one last gasp before the orgasm pulsed through her body.

"Oh, my Lord, Clint. That was . . ."

"Not over yet," he finished.

Clint was already crawling forward again so his hands could slide to the pillow under Katrina's head and his hips could settle in between her legs. Katrina stopped trying to talk and instead pressed her lips against Clint's mouth.

They shared each other's breaths as they tasted each other vigorously. Clint's hands moved along the side of her body, sampling the subtle curves of her waist and breasts. Katrina's hands were busy as well, massaging the muscles on Clint's back.

Once Clint slipped a hand underneath her, he cupped her rounded buttocks and got her in position so he could push his hips forward. His penis slid all the way inside her, delving deep into her until he filled her completely.

Katrina's eyes snapped open and she pulled in a long, shuddering breath. She tightened her grip on him and didn't relax until Clint started moving slowly in and out of her.

In no time at all, their bodies had fallen into the same rhythm. As Clint pumped back and forth, Katrina made little sideways grinding motions that put smiles on both their faces. Clint's hands had closed around Katrina's and he pinned her arms to the bed in a playful yet firm manner.

She looked up at him with excited surprise. That expression became even more powerful as he started thrusting with more force. Now, they let their hunger for each other consume them and they both gave in to the pleasure of sharing each other's bodies.

Now, their bodies were gleaming with sweat and their breaths were becoming more and more labored. Katrina pitched her head from side to side, moaning louder and louder as a second orgasm crept up on her.

Clint thrust into her once again, burying himself inside her. He could feel her body trembling as it had before. This time, however, he let that motion push him over the edge as well. One final thrust was all it took to send them beyond the point of no return.

SIX

Clint woke up to the sound of movement in his room. He opened his eyes to find Katrina padding from one spot to another in her bare feet. Rather than say anything right away, Clint took in the sight of her for a while.

Katrina's slender body looked good in the sparse light of the room and there was just enough of a chill in the air to keep her nipples hard. When she glanced over to see Clint watching her, she jumped back a bit and let out a little yelp.

"You frightened me," she scolded.

Clint was lying on his side and shrugged. "Sorry. I didn't think you were the bashful type."

"You just startled me, is all. How long have you been awake?"

Sitting up, Clint swung his feet over the side of the bed and rubbed his eyes. "Not long. The question I'm more concerned with is how long I've been asleep."

"It's a little after two in the morning," she said.

"And you were going to sneak out without a word?"

"No, it was getting chilly in here, so I thought I'd just—"

Clint got up and stopped her with a quick kiss on the lips. "I was just giving you a hard time," he said. "No need to explain yourself."

The smile on her face shone through even in the shadows that filled the room. Apart from one dying lantern, the only light coming in there was the pale light of the nighttime sky. But it was the time somewhere between late night and early morning, which gave everything a special kind of darkness all its own.

Katrina pulled the piece of clothing she'd found over her head. It was a thin cotton slip and once it dropped over her, the material clung to her in a way that was even better than when she'd been naked. "I thought I might check on my brother," she said. "He was in rough shape the last time I saw him."

The mention of Warren Nolen was like a stiff breeze that almost snuffed out the heat Clint had been feeling. Even so, he managed to sound earnest when he said, "I hope he didn't take it too badly."

"He gambles more than he should. I guess it wouldn't be so bad if he won more often."

"Yeah, that usually does make all those long nights go down a little easier. Does he have a big family to provide for?"

She shrugged. "I was always more worried about his temper. That's what usually gets him into trouble."

"Yeah. I found that out for myself the hard way."

Katrina pouted with her lips and reached out to touch Clint's face. "I hope you didn't get knocked around too badly."

"I came through all right."

"Actually," she whispered as she leaned in close enough for Clint to feel her breath upon his earlobe, "I wish I could've been there to see it. It sounds so exciting."

Clint felt her hands slip around him and he started rubbing her hips. As his hands moved slowly on her, she started swishing her hips back and forth between them. Noticing the pile of clothes on the chair, Clint asked, "How long have you been up?"

One of her hands slid along Clint's stomach and found its way between his legs. "Long enough to start getting ideas again."

Clint could feel himself growing hard as her fingers stroked up and down the length of his cock. "I don't want to keep you from any pressing matters," he said, even as his arms tightened around her.

"Right now I can't think of anything else but you." As she said that, Katrina began rubbing her leg against Clint's.

Feeling the contour of her thigh, Clint eased his hand further down. By the time his hand was under the slip and sampling the smooth, wet lips between her legs, Clint was unable to think of much else either.

Katrina wrapped one arm around the back of Clint's neck and held on tightly. She steered him back toward the bed and then shoved him with both hands until he stumbled and fell onto the mattress. Smiling, she climbed on top of him.

Sitting up on the edge of the bed, Clint held onto Katrina's waist as she eased herself onto his lap. After a bit of shifting, she reached down to guide his cock into her one more time. From there, she lowered herself down the rest of the way until she'd taken him inside her.

Clint locked his fingers at the small of her back so Katrina could lean back as she rode him. She kept her eyes closed and smiled widely while she slid up and down on him. Leaning back a bit more, she shook out her hair so that it flowed over her shoulders and down her back.

Apart from the pleasure she was giving him, Clint was savoring the sight of her on his lap. Her pert breasts stood out as she arched her back. The little dark nipples were hard nubs of dark pink skin. When he leaned forward, Clint took them in his mouth one at a time and alternated between licking them and nibbling gently on the delicate skin.

Before long, Katrina was purring on top of him and moving her hips at a quickening pace. When she was close to another orgasm, she wrapped her arms tightly around him and held on. Her body was so close that Clint could feel the pounding of her heart against his chest.

Clint cupped her buttocks and guided her as he thrust up between her legs. Once again, the sound of her breathy moans filled his ears. Her nails dug into his back and she gasped loudly as her climax raced through her body.

A few more solid thrusts was all it took for Clint to reach that same point and he exploded inside her. When he let go, he found himself almost too weak to sit up.

Katrina curled up next to him on the bed. A few hours later, Clint heard her moving about again. His eyes were too tired to watch her and he didn't want to keep her from whatever she needed to do. Since he didn't trust either one of them once they got their hands on each other, he let her blow a kiss at him and slip out of the room.

SEVEN

When sunlight flooded his room, Clint got up and gathered up his clothes. When he'd first gotten into his room the night before, he'd only wanted to get some sleep and get the hell out of Carte Nueves before anything else happened to him. Now, he was feeling completely different.

His body was still a little tired from their lovemaking and the scent of Katrina's skin still hung like an afterthought in the air. Sometime during the night, she'd stacked his clothes into a neat pile similar to the pile she'd made for herself.

Clint's boots sat next to the pile, which had the heavier belts and gear underneath his pants and shirt. Taking the shirt from the top of the pile, Clint let his mind wander over the wild night he and Katrina had shared.

As he buttoned his shirt, Clint was feeling downright happy. He'd met up with women like Katrina before. They'd run into each other at just the right time and decided to spend a wild night together. Finding her at that particular time had seemed like a blessing. It was just what he needed to put the previous night out of his mind for good.

Just as Clint was wondering if he might meet up with

Katrina for breakfast, he realized that she probably wasn't planning on coming back to his room at all.

Not only was she gone, but all of her clothes were gone as well. That was no big surprise, especially considering how carefully she'd been gathering her things in the darkness hours ago. Thinking back to the sight of her, naked and moving in the shadows, Clint couldn't help but smile. Katrina Nolen was one of those pleasant little surprises that made life worth living.

That contentedness didn't last long in Clint's mind.

In fact, it was chased from him like pheasants being flushed from the bushes when he realized that she wasn't the only thing missing from his room.

"What the hell?" Clint grumbled.

Having gotten to the bottom of his stack of clothes, Clint had nudged his gun belt aside so he could get to his boots. The holster flopped on the floor and skidded a little ways, which had caught his attention immediately. The holster should have been too heavy to move like that.

Feeling his blood race through his veins, Clint grabbed his gun belt and nearly tossed it over his shoulder because it was so light. The leather was familiar in his hand. His fingers knew every crack and every beveled curve. It didn't take that kind of familiarity, however, for him to see that the modified Colt that normally resided in that holster was gone.

A blind man could have realized that much.

With the gun belt dangling from his hand, Clint froze as if his missing Colt was an animal that might be frightened by a sudden move. As his eyes darted about the room, his mind sifted through everything that had happened the night before.

Normally, the modified Colt was never out of reach. Even when he slept or was otherwise occupied, he knew better than to let the gun stray too far from him. His life depended on that gun, but he'd also crafted that gun with his own two hands.

Now that the Colt was out of his sight, he felt anger creep up and start gripping him from the inside. Most of that anger was directed right back at him, which made it that much worse.

In a burst of motion, Clint started tearing the room apart.

The chair was overturned and the rest of the sparse furnishings inside the room were either pushed aside or knocked over completely. The bed was next on his list. After stripping off all the sheets, he lifted the mattress and even picked up the frame so he could get a good look under it.

All he got for his efforts was dusty hands.

As angry as he was, Clint wasn't about to make things worse by giving in to his own frustration. After tugging on his boots, he checked to make sure that his holdout pistol was still in place. Sure enough, the little Colt New Line revolver was stashed in his boot like always. That gun didn't see a quarter of the action of his modified Colt. Instead, it was a weapon that hid and waited until it was needed.

This was one of those times and Clint was real glad to find the pistol in its proper place.

That, however, didn't take the edge off what he was feeling in regard to his missing Colt. Strapping the holster around his waist as a way to fuel his own fire, Clint tucked the New Line into the belt—it didn't fit the empty holster—and stormed out of his room. He was ready for anything ranging from an ambush to an empty hall.

He found the latter.

As before, Katrina Nolen was first and foremost in Clint's thoughts.

This time, he was anything but happy.

EIGHT

"Where'd she go?" Clint asked as he barreled toward the front of the boardinghouse.

There wasn't a desk in the front of the building, but there was a small counter where the woman who ran the place conducted her business. That woman glanced up at Clint and didn't react much until she saw the look burning in his eyes.

"Are you talking about the woman who was here?" the lady asked.

Clint saw the nervousness in the older lady's face and did his best to keep himself from snapping at her. "That's right. The woman who was in my room. Did she come this way?"

The older lady had been seated in a rocker where she was working on knitting something. She got to her feet and carried her needles and the length of unfinished material in her hands. "I don't approve of men bringing women into their rooms," she said sternly. "Married couples are fine, but I'm not running a house of ill repute."

"Tell me where that woman went and I promise I'll leave."

"There are places in town for that sort of thing," she

continued as if Clint hadn't said a word. "And I don't even approve of those. That's why I made sure to run my business away from places like saloons and whorehouses."

On his best day, Clint wouldn't have been content to be lectured by the sour-faced old woman. She'd seemed nice enough when he'd rented the room, but now she was doing everything short of shaking her finger at him.

The old lady set her knitting down and fixed her eyes on Clint. "If you ask me, whatever trouble there is between you two is none of my concern. But I say that, whatever it is, you deserve it," she scolded while shaking her finger at him.

Digging in his pocket, Clint found some money. He reached out to take the old lady's hand and then slapped the money into it. "There you go," he said. "That's for the room and any dirty morals that I subjected you to. Now, can you tell me anything you know about that woman and where she might have gone?"

The old lady stopped right where she was. For a moment, it seemed that she might be scared or upset. Then, after taking a good look at the money Clint had given her, she changed her tune. "The woman isn't from around here," she said while stuffing the money down into the front of her blouse. "She came into town with some other fellow a week ago. I didn't catch any of their names, but I hear they both came from somewhere out west."

"Are you sure about that?"

She nodded. "Between me and the rest of my sewing circle, we know just about everything that goes on around here. The man she was with is some sort of gambler."

"Did you see where she went?"

"She left here a few minutes ago in a real hurry. The way she was looking back at your door, I was thinking she might have been running away from you."

"It's something like that," Clint said, "but not like you might think."

She squinted at him and took a moment to study Clint's

face. All of the innocent sweetness he'd first seen in her was gone. Now, the old lady looked and spoke like someone who'd seen a little bit of just about everything the world had to offer.

"She stole from you?" the old lady asked.

"Yeah."

She nodded. "She struck me as a thieving little tramp."

Clint couldn't help but be a little taken aback by the shift in the lady's tone. An admiring smirk drifted onto his face. "Where'd she go, ma'am?"

"Out the door like a shot and turned left from there. I didn't follow her so I don't know much more than that. You might want to check the Ranch House Hotel. It's where that gambler she was with was staying."

Clint tossed her a wave and headed for the door. As he left, he heard the old lady call out to him in her previous, kindlier voice.

"Be careful, young man."

After that, Clint didn't recall hearing much else. There was activity on the street as locals and newcomers alike all started poking their heads out for breakfast or some other business. There were horses pulling carriages or carrying riders from one place to another, but Clint didn't pay any mind to any of that.

His attention was focused only on where he was headed and what he meant to do once he got there.

Although he couldn't think of a good reason why Katrina would want to steal his gun, it was too suspicious for her to slip away and have something that valuable to him slip out along with her. That Colt might as well have been a piece of Clint's arm. There was no way in hell he would let it go unless it was stolen from him.

Thinking along those lines made him even madder at himself. There was no way in hell he should have allowed anyone to be able to get that Colt away from him.

The truth of the matter was that he'd let his guard

down. It didn't matter how that guard had been lowered or what the circumstances were. All that mattered was that it had happened and he should have known better than to have let it.

By this time, Clint was in sight of the saloon district of Carte Nueves. The place where he'd played cards the night before was across the street and a few other places weren't too far away. The Ranch House Hotel was a little ways down the boardwalk, and Clint practically charged toward that place like he meant to push it over.

It wasn't until the last moment that Clint stopped himself from barging through the door like a madman. After taking a breath, he opened the door and stepped inside in a civilized manner.

"Can I help you?" the clerk behind a long, polished desk asked.

"Is there a Warren Nolen staying here?"

After consulting his register, the clerk nodded. "There sure is."

"What room is he staying in?"

The clerk's eyes narrowed and he studied Clint a little more carefully. "Are you a friend of Mr. Nolen's?"

Clint stepped up to the desk and leaned forward against it. "I sure am. I'm also an acquaintance of his sister's."

"Perhaps I can send him a message?"

One quick glance down was all Clint needed to spot the name and room number scribbled upon the register. "No need for that," he said while storming toward the nearby hallway. "I'll find him myself."

NINE

It felt odd for Clint to have a gun in his hand other than his Colt. The holdout pistol would do well enough if he needed it, but there simply was no substitution for the weapon that felt like a part of himself. Even so, Clint held the smaller pistol at the ready and stood against the wall beside the door.

Carefully, Clint reached out and knocked on the door. After rapping a few times, he pulled his hand back and prepared himself in case the occupants decided to take the easy route and blast a hole through the door itself.

No shot came from inside the room.

In a strange sort of way, Clint was disappointed. At least, if someone had taken a shot at him, he could have busted in there without much hassle. Now, he had to try to get inside the hard way.

Clint was about to knock again. He was even toying with the notion of kicking the door in with a well-placed boot. Before doing any of those things, however, he decided to try things the easy way.

Still keeping his back to the wall, Clint reached out and tried the door's handle. It gave way easily and the door swung open with a gentle nudge.

"I'll be damned," Clint said to himself. "Maybe my luck's set to change, after all."

Clint peeked around the corner, still expecting a storm of lead to greet him at any second. If there was anyone inside that room, they were either real patient or real scared.

In a quick burst of motion, Clint turned the corner and brought his gun up to cover his entrance. His eyes glanced around the room and his ears strained for any hint of someone trying to make their move from inside.

There was nothing in the room apart from the furnishings and a neatly made bed. Clint stepped inside and looked around. He didn't lower his gun until he was certain nobody was in there, hiding and waiting for a chance to strike.

Just as he did lower the gun, Clint heard footsteps behind him. In another burst of speed, Clint spun around and brought the gun up to aim at a petrified old woman.

"I . . . I'm just the cleaning woman," she squeaked.

Her gray hair was tied in a bun at the back of her head. Although her skin was wrinkled, it had a tough, leathery texture that could only come from years of manual labor. Her eyes were sharp, however, and she didn't turn and run after Clint lowered his weapon.

"If you're looking for the ones that were here before," the old woman said, "you're too late. They already left."

"Yeah," Clint replied, taking another glance around the empty room. "I kind of figured that."

She leaned in and lowered her voice to a whisper. "Does the fella from this room owe you money?"

"He owes me, all right. Him and the woman he was traveling with."

"Are you Adams?"

Clint turned to get a better look at her. The instant he saw the twinkle in her eyes and the conspiratorial twitch to her smile, he realized he'd found another member of the Carte Nueves sewing circle. "I sure am."

"What's your first name?"

"Clint."

Nodding, she dug into the pocket of her apron and fished out a folded piece of paper. "Then this must belong to you. I found it on the bed when I was cleaning the room."

"How long ago did you clean this room?"

"No more'n a few minutes. Here," she insisted while pushing the paper at Clint. "Take your message or whatever it is."

Clint took the piece of paper and saw the writing across the front, which simply read, "C. Adams."

It was obvious by the look on her face that the old woman wasn't going to go anywhere without being told to do so. Rather than shoo her away, Clint unfolded the paper and read what was inside.

"See you in Mescall," was all that was written there.

Clint read it a few times, flipped the paper over, and made sure that there wasn't anything else. When he looked up again, the old woman was still staring at him expectantly.

"What's in Mescall?" she asked.

Clint wasn't surprised that she'd read the note. He wouldn't have even been surprised if the old lady at the boardinghouse already knew what it said.

"Guess I'll have to find that out for myself." Tipping his hat to her, Clint left the room.

TEN

It was a short ride back to Labyrinth. He'd been straight-forward when he'd told Katrina about wanting to stretch Eclipse's legs. That was the only thing that had brought him to Carte Nueves and now that he was leaving, Clint wished he would have picked a different direction to ride in the first place.

Maybe then he wouldn't have the knot that was currently in his stomach.

For certain, he would still have his Colt.

Eclipse wasn't at all bothered with Clint's hurry to make it back to Labyrinth. Indeed, the Darley Arabian stallion took it as another opportunity to get a fine bit of exercise. A few snaps of the reins followed up with a touch of heels on the horse's sides sent Eclipse forward like he'd been shot from a cannon.

The miles flew by under the stallion's hooves and his head churned back and forth like the piston on a steam engine. The landscape of West Texas was wide-open and spread out in front of Clint. In no time at all, the first outlines of Labyrinth could be seen on the horizon. Eclipse shifted his course without being told and headed for the stable where he always stayed whenever in town.

Clint greeted the stable boy with a tip of his hat and jumped down from the saddle. He flipped a silver dollar to the kid, confident that the boy knew his job. The saddle was already being unbuckled from Eclipse as Clint left the stable carrying his saddlebags over one shoulder.

Without even making a stop at his usual hotel, Clint headed straight for the saloon owned by his longtime friend Rick Hartman. Rick's Place was a well-known spot in Labyrinth and one of the few places in the country where Clint could go without having to contend with a wagon load of curious drunks wondering if they truly were looking at The Gunsmith himself.

"Hey there, Clint," Hartman shouted as soon as he saw who'd walked through his door. "I was about to get worried that you'd . . . Jesus, you look like you're mad enough to spit."

Clint dropped his saddlebags against the bar and asked, "You ever hear of someone named Warren Nolen?"

Hartman took Clint's abrupt manner in stride. He mulled over that question as he filled a mug with beer and set it on top of the bar. "Warren Nolen? Can't say as that rings any bells."

Grabbing the beer and taking a swig, Clint asked, "What about Katrina Nolen?"

Hartman shook his head. "Nope."

"Figures." As if tasting the beer only after the second sip, Clint let out a relieved breath and held up the mug. "Thanks."

Hartman noticed the subtle change in Clint's manner and decided it was all right to lean against the bar and have a few more words with him. "So, what's got you so fired up? And where the hell have you been for the last day?"

"I took Eclipse for a ride and wound up in Carte Nueves."

"That place is still there?"

"Yep. There's a nice little saloon as well. I got into a

friendly card game and then things took an unfriendly turn."

"All right," Hartman said as he got comfortable where he was standing. "Let's hear about it."

Clint recounted what had happened from the card game on. When he told Hartman that the Colt had been taken from him, the bartender winced.

"How the hell did that happen?" Hartman asked.

"Let's just say I was distracted." Clint took another sip of the beer and recalled Katrina's slender, naked body. "Real distracted."

Hartman nodded and grinned knowingly. "I guess that distraction would be the Katrina Nolen you were asking about?"

"That's her."

"I swear, Clint, someday a lady's gonna be the death of you. Was she at least worth the trouble?"

"Worth the trouble? Not quite." Clint saw the look on Hartman's face and shrugged. "All right. Maybe it was close to being worth it."

Hartman nodded at the concession and asked, "So why come back here? I would've thought you'd chase down that gun of yours all the way to the ends of the earth."

"That might not be necessary." With that, Clint took the folded paper from his pocket and showed it to Hartman. "You know about a town called Mescall?"

Hartman's face already showed that he knew plenty.

ELEVEN

Hartman shifted on his feet so he was good and comfortable before continuing. "First thing I can tell you is that Mescall ain't exactly a town. Well, not in the proper sense of the word."

"What's that supposed to mean?"

"It's more of a camp that gets picked up and moved around whenever it needs to."

"How big of a camp is it?"

"Fairly big. I've been there once and there were enough tents set up to form a few good-sized streets."

"And why would a place need to get moved around?"

Hartman scowled at Clint and asked, "You never heard any of this before?"

"Yeah, Rick," Clint said out of aggravation. "I came all the way back here to pull your leg about some camp."

"All right," Hartman said. "No need to get upset. Sometimes I forget how often you're away from here, is all. Anyway, Mescall was set up to host a few boxing matches a few years ago. Things got out of hand and, as rumor has it, the betting got so fierce that the men who started the matches wanted to keep them out of hand.

"The fights got to be so brutal that the Rangers were

43

coming by to bust them up whenever they could. Rather than fold up their tents for good, the tents were just set up in a different place each time a fight night came along. Word got spread about the underground matches and folks flocked to them like flies to a picnic."

"What kind of boxing matches are these?" Clint asked.

Hartman was already shaking his head. "They're hardly even boxing matches anymore. Now that they're avoiding the law, the promoters decided to go all the way and make the fights really interesting. Anything goes once you step in there. Anything but guns, that is."

"Do you think this has anything to do with my gun being stolen?"

"I can't say for certain," Hartman replied. "But there's a new batch of fights scheduled in the next week or so."

"Is that so?"

"Yep," Hartman said as he knelt down and started rummaging behind his bar. When he straightened up again, he was holding an envelope, which he tossed onto the bar in front of Clint. "That's what it says here on my invitation."

For a moment, Clint thought Hartman had to be joking. Then, after opening the envelope and glancing at what was inside, he looked up at the bartender with disbelief. "You get invitations to these fights?"

"Sure. I own a successful saloon and I can spread the word to a lot of people. And before you say anything else, you should know well enough that these kind of organized brawls aren't anything new. These boys would be knocking each other senseless whether there was a Mescall or not. At least this way, there's some sort of organization."

Clint shook his head. First of all, he was always surprised at how well Hartman knew what was going to come out of Clint's mouth the moment it came into Clint's head. Secondly, he was amazed at the way Hartman came through for him whenever he was needed.

"I suppose you've seen some of these fights for yourself?" Clint asked.

Hartman glanced around and nodded. "I've seen one or two. Hell of a show, if you ask me."

Although his first instinct was to look down on the fights Hartman was talking about, Clint thought about some of the boxing matches he'd seen. Those bouts had been official and had ended with both fighters looking as if a stagecoach had rolled over them.

"I'll assume they weren't too bad," Clint said. "You're not the sort who enjoys watching someone get themselves killed."

"At least you give me a little credit. First of all, the fights are bare-knuckle."

"I've seen a few of those."

"But not like these," Hartman added, visibly getting more excited now that he saw Clint was interested in the subject. "These folks fight like I've never seen. They wrestle, they kick, hell, they even bite if it comes down to it. And if someone in the crowd can slip a bottle or something to one of the fighters, it gets put to good use."

"I've seen a few of those, as well." Clint drained the rest of his beer and laughed. "Come to think of it, I've been in a few of those."

Hartman was laughing as well. Refilling Clint's mug, he said, "I've seen cowboys come into this saloon and plenty others just looking for a fight. The way I see it, let them rowdies fight each other instead of pulling some poor, drunk bastard into the fray."

"Maybe, but the law doesn't quite see it that way."

"Aw, there's a governor or mayor or some sort of politician who's never been out of his mansion that says it's barbaric."

Shrugging, Clint said, "He may have a point, you know."

"True, but hangings in the middle of town square ain't exactly civilized when you get right down to it."

Clint nodded at that. It was something that never did set too well with him, no matter how much a man deserved to swing. Some men might be better off dead, but that didn't mean an audience was necessary.

"By now," Hartman continued, "the fights in Mescall are something of a tradition. I hear that some lawmen even go there to place a bet and make sure things don't spill over outside of the camp."

"Sounds like a nice little system." Looking at Hartman over his beer, Clint asked, "You want to attend?"

"Take in a fight? You can have the invitation if you want. That should be enough to get you in."

"Maybe or maybe not. If whoever stole my gun is going to be there, I don't want to take that chance. What do you say, Rick? Up for a night at the fights?"

TWELVE

Before leaving Labyrinth, Clint paid a visit to a gun shop owned by a man who was one of his longtime admirers. Unlike those who passed along stories of Clint's gunfights, this was a man who respected Clint as a real gunsmith.

While most folks thought Clint had earned his name by the way he handled his gun in a fight, a few knew the real story. Clint was a true gunsmith whose talents were sought after by those who knew that profession. When Clint walked into just about any gun store, he was recognized almost as fast as when he stepped into a high-stakes card game.

This time was no exception.

"Clint Adams! It's been way too long since I saw you come through that door! How you been?"

"Great, Roger, just great." Despite all the concerns on Clint's mind, it was hard to be angry when he was looking at a man as happy as Roger. Roger White was a stout man in his early fifties who had the slender hands of someone born to do delicate work. His eyes were always half shut, mainly because he was always grinning from ear to ear.

Immediately, Roger's eyes darted to the holster at

Clint's hip. "What's the matter, Clint? Afraid I'll talk you out of that splendid Colt of yours?"

"Someone beat you to it, actually."

Roger looked as if he'd been told the sky was falling. "What? Are you joking? Please tell me you're joking."

"It's a long story."

"Did you sell it? If so, I wish I could've had the chance to—"

"I didn't sell it," Clint interrupted. "It was taken from me."

All the color drained from Roger's wide face. "Oh, no!"

"I intend on getting it back, but I'd prefer to have something other than my holdout pistol along for the ride."

"Oh, certainly, certainly," Roger said. Not only had the color returned to his cheeks, but he seemed to be positively beaming. "I'm so glad you came to me, Clint."

The fact of the matter was that there weren't many other gun stores in town, but Clint decided not to bring that up rather than dampen Roger's spirits.

"What can I get for you?" Roger asked as he made his way to a glass case filled with firearms of all shapes and sizes.

Clint walked up to the case and studied every pistol in there. With his expertise in the field, it was all of three or four seconds before he started pointing guns out to the man behind the counter. Roger opened it up and retrieved every one of Clint's selections.

Then, one by one, Clint started testing the guns. He took them in his hand and felt for weight and balance. He held them by the handles and let some of them lie flat across his palms. Through that process, he was able to narrow down the field by half.

As Clint was beginning to examine the remaining half, the door to the shop opened behind him. Rick Hartman stepped inside and moved to stand next to Clint.

"What's going on here?" Hartman asked.

Roger hushed him as if Hartman had interrupted a

church service. "He's deciding on a gun to take along with him."

"Jesus, Clint, I'd say you're the fastest draw I ever seen no matter what gun you're packing. Just pick one and let's get moving."

Clint barely even seemed to notice Hartman was speaking. Instead, he started in on disassembling the guns one at a time until the top of the counter started to look like a junk heap.

"I've got the horses ready to go," Hartman said. "Besides, we're not the ones fighting, remember?"

It seemed as if Clint still wasn't going to answer. Then, without turning away from his task, Clint asked, "You said this event is run outside of the law, right?"

"Well . . . yeah. Technically."

"And there are going to be some of the toughest men you've ever seen there?"

"Oh, yes."

"Then maybe it's not a good idea to go in there without being prepared for the worst. That is," Clint added as he finally looked over to where Hartman was standing, "unless you've gotten good enough to get the drop on these fellows yourself."

Hartman paused for a moment. When he glanced around the room, he spotted Roger White looking very pleased with the situation.

"Okay," Hartman admitted. "Maybe you're right. Just hurry up."

Five minutes later, Clint had taken the best pieces from the best of Roger's stock and fitted them together. Although the parts came from similar makes and models, Clint found the ones with the fewest defects and put together a gun that was better than any single piece in Roger's stock.

"Is that how you built your Colt?" Roger asked.

"Not hardly." Setting the gun he'd put together aside,

Clint put the other guns together until there wasn't a single spare part lying on the counter. "There you go. I think some of these should work out better than before. Of course, there's one that you might want to put on the discount shelf. I guess you might call it the runt of the litter."

Roger's eyes were wide and he put the other guns back in the case. "That may be, Clint, but I'll bet these others will more than make up for it."

"How much do I owe you for this one?" Clint asked as he dug in his pocket for some money.

Roger shook his head as if he was offended by the prospect. "When I say these others will more than make up for it, I mean it. A whole lot more."

Clint nodded and dropped his pistol into his holster. Even though he had used Colt parts, he could feel the difference from the moment he picked up the gun to the instant it fell into place at his side. When he drew it to get a feel for the weapon, his hand was barely visible and the gun emerged with just the slightest brush of iron against leather.

"This'll do," Clint said. "Let's go."

THIRTEEN

Mescall's location was just over a day's ride from Labyrinth. Clint and Hartman knew the area well enough, but there were some parts of West Texas that would never be fully known. The land was too big to be taken lightly and it had a roughness to it that was all its own.

Since they weren't headed for a set location, Clint felt something that he hadn't felt for some time. It felt like they were riding into the unknown, even though they weren't too far from their point of origin.

While some might have been uncomfortable with that feeling in their belly, Clint and Hartman took to it just fine. In fact, it was just what Clint needed to put the smile back onto his face.

"I should've ridden out this way the first time," Clint mused.

Hartman laughed. "Yeah, but then you wouldn't be off on this little goose chase. Sounds to me like meeting up with that lady in Carte Nueves wasn't too bad."

"Sure, right up until she turned into a thief."

"Technically, she was always a thief. You just didn't sniff her out until it was too late."

Clint looked over to find Rick Hartman smirking right

back at him. "I thought you were here to help me," Clint said.

Hartman shrugged. "Maybe I am helping you. Maybe you'll think more next time before you drop your pants and hop into bed with a strange woman."

"Oh, really? And you never got yourself into trouble for that very same thing?"

Clearing his throat and shifting his attention back to the trail ahead of them, Hartman said, "We're not talking about me."

Clint laughed. "I think I just stumbled on something I do want to talk about."

"Shouldn't we go over our plan for when we get to Mescall? It won't be much longer, you know."

"What kind of trouble are you talking about?" Clint asked, doing his damnedest to get Hartman back onto the proper track.

But Hartman would have none of it. "Tell me about them others you played poker with. Maybe they were all in on it."

"I doubt it. In fact, I doubt that the likes of Nate De-Louse could plan a trip across the street without having something go wrong."

Hartman cocked his head to one side. "Wait a second. Who did you just mention?"

Since he'd thrown his last comment out without much thought, Clint had to pause for a moment and go over what he'd said. Finally, he replied, "Nate DeLouse."

"The Louse?"

"You know him?"

"Yeah," Hartman exclaimed. "I tossed that little pisser out of my saloon more than once. The last time wasn't too long ago. He was in Labyrinth during the last time you were away. In fact, he's the one that delivered that invitation I showed you."

"You mean the invitation to the fight?"

Hartman nodded.

"The fight that we're going to right now?"

Again, Hartman nodded. "Small world, ain't it?"

Clint let out a sigh and felt the muscles in his shoulders start to tense up all over again. "And here I thought I wouldn't have to see that stupid smile on his face again."

"You might be seeing that stupid smile pretty soon," Hartman said with a wince. "Nate is in real tight with the ones who run the fights in Mescall. He spreads the word when and where the next fights will be. Odds are that's why he was in Carte Nueves when you ran into him."

Even though Nate wasn't around when his gun had been stolen, Clint had a much easier time picturing the skinny little runt running off with that gun. Then again, a lot of that had to do with the fact that Nate hadn't actually gotten on Clint's good side at all in the times they'd spoken to one another.

"Do you think Nate had anything to do with my gun getting stolen?" Clint asked.

Hartman mulled that over carefully. It seemed that he, too, had to push through the initial response of assuming the worse where Nate was concerned. "Truthfully, I don't see him doing something like that. Nate's a liar and a cheat and he sure as hell is a weasel, but I don't think he's got the sand to sneak into your room and steal the gun from your holster.

"You've got to face up to it, Clint. That pretty girl you took up with caught you with your pants down." Smirking, Hartman added, "No pun intended."

Clint had to shake his head and laugh a bit at that one. "Actually, she was the one who made sure they were down in the first place. Still, this can't be a coincidence. Everyone at that card game has become tied together and I have a hard time believing it was just to steal my pistol. Hell, someone could have bushwhacked me and stolen the damn thing if they wanted it so bad."

Hartman let out a quick, snorting laugh. "Sure, Clint. How many times have you been bushwhacked over the years?"

"More than I can count."

"And how many times have you walked away from it?"

"I'm here, aren't I?"

"My point exactly. Anyone who does a little bit of asking around or digging on you could find out that running up and pissing you off isn't the best of ideas. If I wanted to get something from you, I think I'd have cooked up something like this as well."

"Maybe. But why?" Clint asked. "Why would someone want my gun so badly? They can't think that they can just wave it around and say they killed me. That's insane."

"My friend, I've tended bar for plenty of years. If there's one thing I can tell you for certain, it's that people hardly ever do what they should do. Looking back on it, most of the things they do might be considered insane."

"Good point. I'm just getting tired of trying to put together all the pieces when they all seem so far away."

Hartman smirked and nodded toward the horizon. "Well, it seems they're not as far as you might think. We're almost there."

FOURTEEN

The first thing Clint saw was a jagged series of bumps on the horizon. After studying those bumps a little more carefully, he was able to pick out more distinct shapes. From there, the tops of tents and lean-tos could be seen.

Now that he'd spotted it, the camp seemed hard to miss. The only thing protecting it from being seen in the first place was the way the tops of the structures were all curved in a way that made them blend in with the rest of the hills. Once their horses had carried them just a bit further, Clint and Hartman were able to see the bustling camp known as Mescall.

It was hard to count all the tents. They were clustered together in a way that seemed random from one angle, but completely ordered from another. Once Clint and Hartman were riding on the trail that led straight into the camp, they could easily see the way the tents were arranged in rows.

Just as Hartman had said, there were pathways between the tents that resembled streets. Clint had been to some big mining camps before, but this one was enough to impress him. Mainly, that was due to the fact that he'd been through this part of Texas not too long ago and the camp had been nowhere to be seen.

It was there now, however. Nobody with their wits about them could say any different. And now that he was approaching Mescall, Clint could sense that the people he was after were nearby.

"Quite a place, huh?" Hartman asked. "I told you it was big."

Clint nodded, taking in the sights and sounds that were all around him. Not only were there plenty of people moving about, but there were even sounds of blacksmiths and carpenters plying their trades. If he closed his eyes, Clint might have thought that he was in a real town.

Closer inspection of the place was enough to dispel that illusion, however. Unlike a town or even a mining camp, Mescall was clearly not meant to stay in one place. The tents all wobbled in the breeze and the wooden frames all creaked as if they would collapse at any moment.

The paths between the tents hadn't even been used frequently enough to develop ruts. Instead, short grass and rocky soil made every step bumpy and every floor uneven. Despite its flaws, Mescall seemed to be downright prosperous.

Clint couldn't look from one spot to another without seeing at least a dozen new faces. People flowed through the camp like blood through a heart, every last one of them bumping into one another or dodging each other with skill perfected from spending too much time in close quarters.

Although all of them glanced up at Clint and Hartman, it was more of a way to keep from being stepped on by the horses than anything else. There were too many people about for anyone to be concerned with new arrivals. As if the crowds weren't enough, there was plenty more to capture folks' attention.

Barkers shouted out from stalls or open-ended wagons set up anywhere there was space. They sold everything from snake oil to imported suits and they advertised by way of screaming, poking, and harassing anyone who stepped close enough for them to do so.

Hartman looked down at the salesmen, drunks, and cowboys from his saddle. The amused smile that had come onto his face upon entering Mescall was growing by the second. "Hell of a place, huh, Clint?"

Although Clint was impressed with the size of the camp, all the activity around him felt like static crackling in the air before a storm. "Yeah. Where do we put up the horses?"

"I'm not sure. This place ain't anything like the last time I was—"

"Horses?" came a voice, interrupting Hartman in mid-sentence. "You need a place for your horses?"

The one who'd cut in was an anxious man in his twenties. His hair resembled black straw that had been pasted to his scalp and his grubby hands were already reaching up for Clint and Hartman's reins. "I know a place for your horses," the young man said. "Best place here. Fresh straw. Good prices. I'll take you there."

Clint waved him off and said, "We'll find a place for ourselves."

As soon as the young man left, another two took his place. They descended upon Clint and Hartman like vultures fighting over a scrap of meat.

"Does any of this look familiar?" Clint asked, doing his best to avoid the clamoring barkers and keep Eclipse from getting too nervous.

Hartman looked around like he was at a carnival. "In a way it does, but then it doesn't. This is what it was like, but the setup is different."

"Well, no matter what the setup is, I'd wager there are stables toward the edge of camp. Let's head over there," Clint said while pointing to one of the less crowded corners in sight. "At least there we can get a moment to hear ourselves think."

After riding past a few shanty corrals that weren't much more than empty bits of ground sectioned off by rope, Clint settled on a spot for himself. It wasn't a proper stable and might not have even been inside Mescall. It was a patch of quiet land that he could see without going too far from the thick of things.

Rather than favor any of the obnoxious scouts looking to drag the horses into one dirty stall or another, Clint bought a lean-to for himself and set it up on the land he'd spotted. Eclipse and Hartman's horse fitted nicely under there and seemed relieved to be away from the noises of Mescall.

Unfortunately, Clint wasn't so lucky.

Once Clint and Hartman were on their own two feet, the crowds of Mescall seemed to double in size. The two men were unable to look over all those heads, and the bodies pressed in on them from all sides. After being on the open range, Clint felt especially nervous with so many folks stumbling into him.

"Where're the fights held?" Clint asked impatiently. "Or, more importantly, where can we go to find Katrina? I wouldn't mind getting through with this and getting out of here."

"Out of here?" Hartman asked. "Why would you want that? Come on, Clint, I thought you liked to be in the thick of things."

"This is a mess," Clint replied. At the sound of shouting voices, Clint turned, and was just able to step to one side to avoid a pair of fighting drunks before they knocked him over. Once they'd passed him by, the men kept fighting and staggered toward the next unlucky soul. "And a violent mess at that."

"You've been to enough new towns to know that you got to walk around a place for a while and get a feel for it. By the time we ask for directions, we could have just seen it all for ourselves. This place ain't too big for that."

"You're right. I'm just starting to get the feeling that we're letting whoever stole my gun get farther and farther away. I mean, what if they're not even here?"

"The note said they would see you in Mescall, right?" Hartman asked.

"Yeah."

"Well, this is Mescall. What else do you want?"

"I want to find whoever's got my gun and wring their neck," Clint grumbled. "That's what I want."

"Aw, you just need a drink." Hartman pointed to one of the tents they were approaching and said, "Here's our first stop."

Looking in the direction Hartman was pointing, Clint saw a wooden sign hanging from a bent nail over a crooked door frame that read, BEER GARDEN.

FIFTEEN

Clint's hopes of finding a bartender with some answers were dashed the moment he walked into the beer garden. Rather than a proper saloon, the garden was more of a watering hole where men walked in one end and were herded out the other. In a matter of two minutes, Clint and Hartman were outside again with dented tin mugs of beer in their hands. They were out of there so quickly that they barely remembered being in.

Once he saw what had happened, Hartman glanced down at the mug in his hand and lifted it to his mouth. He took one careful sip and then spit it out. "Aw, Jesus," he groaned before dumping out the rest. "I can't believe I paid for this."

Clint took a sip of his own beer. The brew was a nasty mix of bitter and sweet. The bitter came from what had to be salt, and he didn't even want to think about where the sweet came from. "That's it," he said while turning over his mug so the rest of his beer could join Hartman's on the ground. "We came all this way, so I'm not going to get shoved from one tent to the other. Where were the fights held when you were here last time?"

60

"They were in a pit with a roof over it. Some were held in the open, but most of them were in that pit."

Nodding, Clint pushed his way through the crowd until he spotted a face that seemed more anxious to meet his eyes than look away. "When are the fights?" Clint practically shouted.

In much the same manner as when he'd mentioned looking for a stable, Clint's request was met by several eager barkers. This time, however, the response was even greater and Clint was soon overwhelmed with grubby hands shoving programs, schedules, betting tables, and odds charts in his face.

It didn't take long for Clint to fall into a rhythm that matched the speed of the barkers' offers. Clint's voice rattled right along with the rest of them, going through a frenetic bargaining process until he finally wound up with several samples of the barkers' wares.

Hartman stood to the side, watching Clint go. When it was over, he shook his head as though the entire process had made him dizzy. "Good Lord," Hartman said. "I didn't know you could talk that fast."

Clint merely shrugged. "When in Rome. Help me go through this stuff. I think there's a map in here somewhere."

The map Clint was referring to was more of a sketch that had been scribbled onto the back of a piece of rumpled newsprint. When they looked at that simplistic drawing, the camp was even easier to figure out.

Mescall was basically made up of a few key pieces. There were places to eat, places to sleep, places to fight, and places for horses. Each section was kept separate, with salesmen's carts and wagons scattered throughout the mix.

The map in Clint's hand showed how each section was arranged. Once they got an idea of which way they were facing, they figured out where everything was. With that bit of knowledge, Mescall suddenly became a whole lot more manageable.

"This is pretty close to the last time I was here," Hartman said. "Only the sections were arranged differently."

"Makes sense," Clint said. "Since they're on the move so much, they just put the pieces together however it suits them when they get to their new spot. Not a bad system, really."

"Kind of like a gypsy caravan, only bigger."

Clint looked around and thought of it from that perspective. "All right. I think I should be able to make some sense of this after all."

"You see? I told you all you needed was a drink."

Just the mention of that brought the sweet, bitter taste back into Clint's mouth and a wince to his face.

Hartman was getting the same sort of look on his own face. "Well, it got us moving in the right direction, anyway."

"Yeah, well, I think the right direction is right through there," Clint said as he pointed to a lane that wound its way between two rows of leaning tents.

As they walked, they could feel they were on the right track. Although there were a few women around, most of them were keeping their heads down and trying not to be noticed. That wasn't too surprising considering that the majority of the people there were men and they were rowdy as hell.

There was a spark in the air that only came about at a fight. Clint had felt it at boxing matches and saloons that were known for having more blood on the floor than beer in their mugs. Before long, Clint could feel that tension working its way through his own system as well.

"This is great," Hartman said, obviously feeling the effects for himself.

"It's different, I'll give you that. So how does this work, anyway? Where are the bets placed?"

"There are booths set up near each fight. There's also

runners who'll take bets and hand out tickets. Just be sure to get a runner you recognize, since there are a few of 'em who'll just run off with your money. I found that out the hard way last time."

"And where's all the money kept?"

"What money?"

"To cover the bets," Clint said, trying to pull Hartman's attention away from the chaos all around him. "There's got to be somewhere the gambling money is kept. Just like there's a place where the profits from this whole place are kept. Most of the stores look independent, but they can't all be that way. That beer garden sure as hell can't be independent or it would've been run out by some other place that doesn't serve frothy piss in a mug."

"Now that you mention it, there were a whole lot of armed men standing guard around a wagon. Like I said, though, this place is laid out differently than when I was here last time."

"Where was the wagon?"

"Ummm, it was in between the two fighting spots. Between the pit and a ring set up in the open."

"The whole may not be the same, but the pieces probably are," Clint pointed out. "Let's put that theory to the test right now."

SIXTEEN

The wagon was small and sat in its spot like a brick that had settled into the ground after a rain. Its wheels were firmly entrenched into the dirt and the harness was also wedged against the ground, making it seem even more immovable.

It resembled a small train car in that it was a squat rectangle of solid construction. Despite the grime covering most of the wagon from top to bottom, it seemed to be the best-maintained structure in Mescall. There were no markings on the side of the wagon and nothing written on the narrow door leading into the back.

Maybe twice the size of a stagecoach, the wagon had twice the amount of guards watching it that a good-sized bank would. There were at least a dozen armed men watching the perimeter. The farthest any of those men got from the wagon was about ten paces, while most of them were close enough to reach out and touch it.

Although the wagon was in a fairly secluded area, there wasn't much within Mescall's boundaries that could be considered quiet. People walked by constantly, talking loudly and carrying on as they went from one tent to another. The squat, heavy wagon was kept away from most of it and the guards discouraged anyone else from getting much closer.

Those guards weren't quite so successful with everyone.

"What's this over here?" came a booming voice from the nearby throng of people.

A few of the guards shifted their eyes in that direction to find a big man swaggering forward.

Rick Hartman wasn't drunk, but he'd seen men under the influence more than enough to make a good show of it. His steps had the power and confidence of someone who didn't know any better. The look on his face made it plain to see that he was going to be a handful.

"This looks good," Hartman bellowed. "What you boys got in there?"

One of the guards on the perimeter stepped out and made sure the shotgun cradled in his arm was easy to see. "Ain't nothing to see here, friend. Keep moving."

Hartman's eyes widened and he let out a low whistle. "Must be good if it's got all you boys waiting to get in. Come on, now. Just tell me what's in there."

The guard with the shotgun reached out to push Hartman back. He was also being joined by a few of the other nearby guards. "I said move it along. Can't you see you're not wanted here?"

"Well, I got my invite right here," Hartman said impatiently as he waved his envelope around. "That means I can see what's going on here. I can handle any women you got in there or any drinks you're serving, so just step aside."

"I said move along. Don't make us get rough with you."

"Hey! No call for that. If you want to get rough, I can make you wish you weren't never born."

Clint smirked and shook his head as he watched Hartman at work. There was just enough of a slur in Hartman's voice to make him seem a little drunk and just enough of a snarl to make him seem a little dangerous. The combination was working beautifully and was drawing enough of the guards away to create a hole for Clint to slip through.

Making sure to keep his head low and his steps quiet, Clint maneuvered around the wagon and to the gap left by some guards who were now dealing with Hartman. The door leading into the wagon was still inaccessible, but Clint was able to make his way up to one of the small square windows along the side.

The window was too high for Clint to get a look inside. Just to make sure, he glanced around to see how Hartman was doing in maintaining his distraction.

Although he hadn't pulled any more guards to him, he was still doing a real good job of occupying the ones around him. In fact, it seemed that all of the guards were looking that way, which at least allowed Clint to move in close enough to press his back against the wagon just below the open window.

"Get yer hands offa me!" Hartman hollered. "I'll have you know that I can make your lives real miserable if I choose to!"

"Yeah, yeah," one of the other guards replied. "Just step back, for Chrissake."

As much as Clint wanted to watch the show Hartman was putting on, he forced himself to concentrate on what was going on inside the wagon instead. It took a little doing, but now that he was leaning against the wagon and directly beneath the window, he could start to hear muffled voices from inside.

". . . the hell is going on out there?" said a gruff voice that had to be coming from someone just on the other side of the wall where Clint was standing.

The next voice was weaker, but distinct enough for Clint to pick up on it right away.

"Weeeell, I'd say there's a little commotion out there," Nate said in his unmistakably grating tone.

The wagon rocked a bit and bumped against Clint's shoulder as someone moved inside. To get the wagon moving like that, Clint knew that the other person in there was a hell of a lot bigger than Nate DeLouse.

"Either tell me what you see or get away from the window," the other man snarled from inside the wagon.

"Ehhhh, looks like it's just some drunk. I'd say things are well in hand."

"Good. Now, where were we?"

The wagon rocked a bit more and Clint could feel it as the big man leaned back against the same wall where he was standing.

"Dilkins," Nate said.

Clint could hear some shifting, followed by the rumble of the second man's voice.

"Dilkins. Right. It's Dilkins in the third. Werner is second. And we've got Offermann in the fourth. How many is that?"

"Ehhhh, looks like all eight to me."

"Good. What about our Grand Prize?"

"Still in the safe, Mr. Hackett. You want me to check it?"

"I'll check it myself when I make the deposit. If it's not in there, I'll just have to skin your sorry ass and throw you to the wolves."

Nate's laugh sounded forced and very uncomfortable. Even through the thick walls of the wagon, Clint could practically feel the fear coursing through DeLouse's veins.

"I'm not joking, Louse," the second man snarled. "Now get out of here and tell the guards to either shoot that damn drunk or get him the hell away from here."

Nate's steps sounded like tapping compared to the heavier ones from before. Clint was moving away from the wagon before the door even began to shift in its frame. By the time the door opened and Nate stepped down, Clint was well out of sight.

"I, ehhhh, don't think Mr. Hackett is too happy with all the noise," Nate said to the closest guard.

"That drunk's leaving," the guard replied. "Don't get all riled up, Louse."

"It's DeLouse," Nate corrected. "Pronounced 'Dee Loose.'"

"What?"

"Forget it."

Nate ambled off, muttering to himself in disgust. Clint and Hartman were already gone.

SEVENTEEN

Since the most crowded place in the entire camp was the section that served the most liquor, that was where Clint met up with Hartman after splitting up near the wagon. Hartman was already waiting there with a smug look on his face when Clint came along.

"You owe me a beer," Hartman said. "In fact, I'd say you owe me all the beers I drink while we're here for making me go in there like that. I nearly got my head knocked off."

"I saw the whole thing," Clint said. "You were playing it up like you were born on a stage."

"Yeah, well, those guards were still about to get rough. I think they were getting ready to throw some punches."

Thinking back to the last order the man inside the wagon had given, Clint let out a wary chuckle. "You don't know the half of it."

"What was that?"

"Nothing. I'll buy you that beer and we can go over what I heard."

Now that they knew where to look, Clint and Hartman were able to find a place much better than the supposed garden they'd been to before. The largest of the camp's saloons was a large tent with a long row of stacked boxes that passed for a bar. After getting their drinks, the two of them crouched over a small round table nailed into a post.

The table wasn't much more than a ring of wood at waist level. Since there wasn't a chair to be found, Clint guessed they were meant to stand. Hartman stood next to him and looked around while nodding his head.

"I'll bet this place turns a nice little profit," Hartman said.

"You might not want to take any business tips from anyone around here," Clint warned.

"I know, but it must be nice to run a place without ever having to worry about fixing a leaky roof or replacing broken chairs."

"You want to see about buying an interest in this place or should we talk about why we're here?"

"No need to bite my head off." Taking a sip of his beer caused Hartman to wince and then nod approvingly. "Go on and fill me in."

Clint took a sip and felt a definite kick to the brew. He couldn't quite put his finger on it, but there was something else in the beer apart from the normal ingredients. It had to have been some sort of harder liquor that put the fire into the back of Clint's throat.

"I think we just found out why everyone's so rowdy around here," Clint said.

"Another smart move where a fight's taking place. You know, from a business standpoint."

Clint recounted the conversation he'd overheard and Hartman listened while sipping his spiked beer. While he left out the part where the man inside the wagon had ordered his men to shoot Hartman if he wouldn't shut up, Clint did hit all the major points.

"Does the name Hackett mean anything to you?" Clint asked.

After thinking it over, Hartman nodded. "Yeah, I think there's a Hackett who runs this show."

"Makes sense. You know anything about him?"

"Just that he used to be a fighter himself. He's always looking for business owners to go in with him on this venture. And," Hartman added while hefting his mug, "the man knows his beer."

"What did you say about him talking to business owners?"

"He was looking for partners," Hartman explained. "At least, he was when I was here last time. By the looks of how much this place has grown, I'd say he found a few good ones. I was asked to come aboard, but it didn't sound like something I wanted to get wrapped up in. Now, if it was a proper venture without the hassle from the law, I might consider it."

"If it was a proper venture, it probably wouldn't be so successful."

"Good point. Folks do tend to enjoy going where they're not supposed to go."

Clint took another sip of the beer and found it was starting to go down much easier every time he tried it. He could see why it was so popular among the rest of the camp. "The first fight should start in a few hours," he said. "At least, that's what was on the overpriced schedule we bought."

"It starts at seven sharp," Hartman clarified. "I saw a notice when I was being roughed up by those guards."

"Then that gives us some time to get a feel for the rest of this place before things really heat up. I have a feeling that once these cowboys see some heads get cracked, they'll be raising some hell of their own."

"We should split up and try looking for Katrina or that brother of hers. If they're around here, it'll be a whole lot easier to find them as opposed to when this place starts to burst at the seams with drunken brawlers."

"My point exactly. Let's split up and meet back at the seven o'clock fight. Did you get a look at Nate back at the wagon?"

Hartman nodded.

"Then you look for him and I'll search for those other two."

"All right, but I want you to promise me one thing."

"What's that?" Clint asked.

"I want you to watch your step around here. I got a good, close look at those guards and I can tell you they're not playing around. They were close to hurting me and I was just shooting my mouth off. Lord only knows what they'll do if they catch you where you're not supposed to be."

Clint nodded and took one last sip of his beer. "Point taken. But I have a feeling that there's more going on around here than just some fights. Maybe one of us can figure what that is with a little poking around. At the very least, Nate should know something."

Hartman started to leave, but then stopped. "Speaking of Nate, what should I do if I find him?"

"Ask him what he knows about a gun being stolen. He shouldn't recognize you, so maybe you can get him to say more than he should. After that, try to set up a meet with him or offer to buy him a beer. That way, we might be able to rope him into being at a certain place at a certain time."

"I guess that's the next best thing to hog-tying him and stuffing him in a sack somewhere."

"Maybe so, but let's not put that option completely out of our minds."

EIGHTEEN

Since most of the faces Clint spotted within Mescall were dirty, scowling, and male, it wasn't too hard at all to pick out the females in the crowd. Considering the pretty face belonging to Katrina Nolen, he figured that he had an even easier task than Hartman in trying to find her as opposed to anyone else.

Of course, just because she should have been easier to spot didn't mean that Clint picked her out right away. Simply getting from one spot to another was a chore as the time for the next fight drew near. According to the schedule, there had been fights going on for a few days already. The main tournament, however, wasn't supposed to start until tomorrow. Most of the other fights were to earn a spot in the main one, which supposedly led to the biggest prize of the bunch.

As far as Clint was concerned, all of that affected him only in how the fights would shift the crowds. He could move around easier between the fights since there was more of a crowd to use for cover. On the other hand, during the fights, the other parts of Mescall should be much emptier and easier to navigate.

As he was thinking about all of this, Clint was weaving

73

through the crowd with growing efficiency. He nearly tripped over a couple sets of boots, however, when he found his eyes being drawn to a wide tent about twenty yards away.

The tent wasn't marked, but it was in the section of Mescall that was set aside for renting beds for the night. What had caught Clint's eye was a tail of blond hair coming from the back of a kerchief tied around a woman's head. That woman had the build and slender frame that Clint had gotten to know very well in Carte Nueves.

Like a hunter who'd finally caught sight of his prey, Clint felt his heart pound in his chest and his breath speed up. As much as he wanted to rush after her, he held back and contented himself with merely keeping her in his sight.

The blonde was headed from one large tent to another and doing a good job of keeping her face out of plain view. She needed to look up at the small sign upon the tent where she stopped, however, which was exactly what Clint had been waiting for.

It was Katrina, all right. After reading the words scrawled onto the sign over the entrance, she ducked her head and stepped inside.

Once Katrina was through the door, Clint picked up his own pace and started hurrying to follow her. Just as he was getting close enough to read the sign that Katrina had looked at, Clint felt something jab into his ribs.

Rather than stop and see who'd knocked into him, Clint stepped in the opposite direction so he could get by. But that way had been blocked as well and he found that out the moment he bounced against a solid wall of flesh and bone.

"Watch where you're going, little man."

Coming from just about anyone, those words couldn't have been anything but an insult when aimed in Clint's direction. But coming from the giant that blocked Clint's path at the moment, the words seemed to fit all too well.

Clint did look like a little man when compared to the

burly tower dressed in jeans and a cotton shirt. The shirt was unbuttoned halfway, but looked as if it might have been busted open by the muscles of the man wearing it. Huge, apelike arms hung down to his sides as he stared down from a good nine or ten inches over Clint's head.

Turning to get a look at the giant, Clint couldn't help but keep his astonishment from showing on his face. "That's, uh, my mistake."

The giant was smiling. It was an expression that didn't seem to fit on his head, which was shaved clean to look like a boulder that had been pulled up from a river and set upon his shoulders. "Then don't let it happen again."

With that, the giant pushed Clint aside and kept walking.

Watching the giant move along was as easy as keeping track of a buffalo as it walked through short grass. Once he saw the giant turn a corner and disappear, Clint started walking toward the tent where Katrina had gone.

A few feet from the entrance, Clint felt another sharp jab to the ribs. This time, it was followed up by a slap on the shoulder and he was forcefully pulled around 180 degrees.

"All right, Gunsmith," said a man with a dirty, leering face, "let's see how tough you are!"

NINETEEN

The first punch came so quickly that Clint didn't even see it. He had no trouble telling where it landed once he felt the impact in the middle of his stomach. Doubling over a bit, he sucked in a painful breath while pushing forward off both legs.

Clint's charge was short and sweet, ending with him driving a shoulder into the torso of the man who'd cold-cocked him.

Like sharks responding to a drop of spilled blood, the rest of the crowd turned on their heels and stepped back to give the fighters some room. Although that brought a whole mess of unwanted attention right to Clint's face, it allowed him to get a clearer view of the men who'd decided to take a swing at him.

There were three of them in all. The one who'd thrown the first punch was still catching his breath and straightening up after Clint's response. The other two were a little smaller, but wiry. All three of them had wild eyes and fidgeting hands that drifted a little too close to their guns.

"'Been following you since Labyrinth," the leader of the three said. "Heard you lost a little somethin', Adams.

Lost that fancy gun of yours and I think you ain't nothing without it."

Hearing that, Clint moved his hand reflexively to the holster at his side. The gun he'd pieced together was still there, but it wasn't the Colt that he should have felt in that spot. He forced himself not to bother trying to figure out how long it had taken word to spread out of Roger White's gun shop.

"Who are you?" Clint asked.

One of the other two snapped his head forward as if that would be enough to bait Clint into making a move. "We're the ones that're gonna kill us a legend," he said through a cocky grin. "And we even got us a nice, big audience."

"I don't know what you three heard," Clint lied. "But I'm not out to fight anyone here."

The three punks fanned out and stood their ground. The one who'd punched Clint stood in the middle with his friends on either side.

"You best fight, Gunsmith," the one in the middle said, tossing Clint's name around for maximum effect. "Or we'll just gun you down. Either way, we get known for taking you down. I think maybe you're all talk and a fancy shooting iron. Let's see how tough you are now that the odds are leveled."

Clint was losing his patience. Not only was everyone staring at him, but they were hearing his name echoing throughout Mescall. All he could picture in his mind was Katrina scooting off to another place where Clint would never find her.

"Hell," the gunman on the right of the middle snorted. "With a fancy gun like that, I bet any one'a us could shoot like you."

Letting out a breath, Clint stopped thinking about Katrina and forced himself to accept what had happened. "All right, then," he said evenly. "It seems like you boys know something about me. I'd like to hear where you got your information, but it only takes one of you to talk. That means I don't much need the rest of you."

The punks on either side of the middle glanced in at the biggest of the three. The nervousness in their eyes might as well have been written across their faces. It caused them to shift on their feet and lick their lips while flexing their fingers.

"Don't listen to him," the one in the middle said without taking his eyes off Clint. "Let's just do what we came to do."

"Sure," Clint said. "The only question is, which of you wants to go first?"

The crowd held its collective breath and waited to see what was going to happen next. The only sound that was made came from the rest of Mescall that wasn't watching the showdown between Clint and his three attackers. Because of the thick masses of people stuffed into Mescall, it seemed that only those in the immediate vicinity knew what was going on.

That immediate vicinity, however, was Clint's entire world.

If nobody in the crowd was making an aggressive move, Clint wasn't bothering with them. If there was somebody hiding in that crowd to take a shot at him, he would just have to wait until he could do something about it. For now, he studied every twitch on the three punks' faces.

He watched every shift of their eyes.

He took in every detail of their faces until finally one of them made his last mistake.

The one on the far right flinched as if he'd hiccuped, and made a grab for his gun.

Clint reacted and reached for the pistol at his side. The instant his fingers touched the weapon, he recognized it as different than the one he was accustomed to. And it wasn't until he was pulling the gun from its holster that he realized he'd forgotten one thing.

The sights.

He'd forgotten to file the sights down, and now they were scraping against the inside of Clint's holster like fingernails hanging onto the edge of a cliff. Clint gritted his teeth as he cleared leather, feeling as though he'd been just as hobbled as the other three figured he was.

He was off by at least a quarter of a second, which had almost given the man in front of him a fighting chance.

Aiming at the hip, Clint squeezed his trigger and felt the gun buck against his palm. The bullet flew a little higher than he was used to, just as it had when he'd tested the gun on his way from Labyrinth. Unfortunately, old habits died hard and Clint had forgotten to adjust his aim.

The gunman on the right was knocked back as hot lead punched a hole through his collarbone. He grunted and reeled backward as his feet came out from under him, hitting the ground hard in a sprawling mass of flailing limbs.

As Clint shifted his aim to the remaining two men in front of him, he made a note to himself on how the gun had felt when it fired. In the blink of an eye, he calculated the recoil and accuracy of his shot the way an accountant might balance a ledger.

The gunman on the left gaped at his fallen partner and started to shake in his boots. His eyes darted back and forth between Clint and the man writhing on the ground as his mouth opened and closed without being able to push out a single word.

Seeing that one man was too panicked to move, Clint looked to the one in the middle of the three men. That one was already dropping to one knee and squeezing his trigger to fire in Clint's direction.

The shot went high and to one side, mostly due to the way the man had moved as he pulled his trigger.

Clint didn't even wince as the wild bullet hissed past him. Instead, he aimed and calmly squeezed his own trigger. The pistol barked once more and sent its shot right where Clint had intended.

Twitching and blinking in surprise, the man in the middle of the three let his jaw drop open and his breath seep from his lungs. The bullet had passed through his skull so quickly that he hardly even noticed. In fact, he seemed surprised that he no longer had the strength to lift his gun anymore. When he crumpled over, he barely seemed to realize why he was falling.

Now that both of his partners had fallen, the last remaining gunman didn't want any part of the fight they'd started. He dropped his gun as if had bitten him and turned to run away. He made it all of two steps before he slammed into a pair of men standing behind him. They were both holding shotguns and one of those shotguns was delivered, butt-first, into the gunman's chin.

The panicked gunman hit the ground with a whimper.

Clint eased his pistol back into its holster as the men who'd been guarding Mr. Hackett's wagon emerged from the crowd. Their faces were unreadable, but Clint was prepared for the worst.

TWENTY

"Looks like someone don't know about the rules around here."

Those words drifted through the crowd from behind the guards. Two of the shotgunners stepped aside to let another man step between them. They closed ranks the moment the other had passed them by.

The man who showed himself looked as though he'd been built from logs fixed onto a barrel. His rounded torso was so thick that it looked like it could withstand a barrage of shotgun blasts. His squat legs were just as solid and didn't even seem to bend in the middle. Thick arms hung down and to the side, unable to hang straight due to the mass of his upper body.

Although Clint hadn't seen the man's face, he recognized the booming voice immediately as the one he'd heard in that wagon not too long ago. That voice emanated from a head the size of an overripe melon. A half circle of dark hair started at the back of one ear and wrapped around to the back of the other ear.

Looking down at the three scruffy gunmen, the barrel-chested man nodded and smirked. "I know better than to ask for men to put up their guns before coming to my fights," he said from beneath a mustache that would have been more at home on a walrus. "But I expect them to keep from shooting 'em off while they're in Mescall."

The gunman in the middle of the three lay sprawled out where Clint had dropped him. His surprised expression was still intact upon a face that had been given a third eye. The one on the right was trying to get up and clutching a hand to the messy wound on his shoulder. The last one had gotten to his feet and was trying to talk even though his jaw was swollen and possibly broken.

"We'll leave, Misher Acket," the gunman pleaded through his wounded jaw. "You won' never shee ush again."

The barrel-chested man nodded at the man while flashing him a condescending smile. "You know who I am, then?"

"Yesh, shir!"

"Then you must have also known my rules. Right?"

"Yesh. I mean . . ." His eyes darted around to take in the shotgunners closing in around him while he racked his brain to come up with a way to get himself out of that spot in one piece.

"What would make you want to come in here and kick up this mess?"

The gunman with the broken jaw was still struggling to get out of the hole he was in. That, combined with the pain shooting through his face and neck, practically crippled him.

"What about you?" the barrel-chested man asked as he turned to the gunman with the wounded shoulder. "You mind telling us what the hell brought you in here with your guns blazing?"

Clint had intended on stepping in, but he was just as interested in hearing what his scruffy attackers had to say.

Gritting his teeth, the other surviving gunman pressed a hand against the wound on his shoulder. His hand, neck, and shoulder were coated in thick layers of wet crimson.

"We heard from a man in Labyrinth . . . heard that Adams was here and was ripe for the picking."

"So you three decided to prove yourselves here and now? Three against one? When you thought that one was at a disadvantage?"

Although neither of the two gunmen replied, the looks on their faces spoke volumes.

"Someone remind these sorry sons of bitches what happens when they break my rules."

With that, two of the shotgunners stepped forward. They pointed their weapons at the man with the broken jaw and pulled their triggers within a heartbeat of one another.

One blast would have been enough to put the gunman out of his misery. Two of them nearly cut him in half.

"Hold on!" Clint shouted.

But it was too late for anyone to do anything. The order had been given and before Clint could make a move, a third shotgun blast roared through the air. This time, the blast was aimed at the man whose shoulder had been wounded and it carved a sizable chunk out from the top of his head.

Smiling like a farmer walking through a field of tall corn, the barrel-chested man stepped up to Clint and extended his hand. "The name's Dale Hackett. You've got my apologies for the trouble you were caused here today."

Clint didn't shake Hackett's hand voluntarily. Instead, his hand was swept up by the bigger man and engulfed before he could do much about it.

"My guests come here for a good time," Hackett said. "I aim to make sure they get it without having to worry about this sort of thing." Looking around to the crowd, he added, "I mean, you men are here to watch fights, not be in them. Am I right?"

Hackett was given a rousing cheer from the crowd that had gathered to see the sparks fly. Now that it was over, a good number of the crowd were already moving on to more exciting things.

Glancing back at his guards, Hackett said, "Someone clean up this mess."

A couple of the shotgunners moved to do just that, picking up the bodies like they were so much garbage.

"Did I hear them right?" Hackett asked after shifting his eyes back to Clint. "Are you really Clint Adams?"

Clint nodded. "Yeah. You heard right. That also means you must have been listening for a while before the shooting ever started. That seems odd for someone who wants to enforce any degree of order."

Hackett smirked and lowered his voice. "I don't prefer this sort of thing, but it was one hell of a show. Besides, I find it necessary to set an example like this every time I put on these fights. I'm sure you'll find folks less willing to wave their guns about from now on."

"I appreciate the concern," Clint said. "But I can handle myself just fine. Actually, I'm sure those other two would've scampered off well enough without having to be blasted to hell in the process."

"Fine talk coming from a known gunfighter," Hackett shot back. Before allowing his words to sink in too far, he stepped back and bowed his head slightly. "No insult meant, Adams. I guess my temper's running a little on the hot side. If there's anything I can do for you, just let me know."

With that, Hackett turned and started walking back to the guards who hadn't disappeared with the bodies of those three gunmen.

The guards cleared a path for Hackett with the meanness in their eyes that had nothing at all to do with the shotguns they carried. They dared any of the drunks in the crowd to step up to them and got no takers. When Hackett moved past them, he patted his guards on the shoulders the way he might pat a dog on its head.

As the crowd went back to its normal flow, it receded from Clint and the spot where the other three gunmen had made their stand. Now that he could see more of his surroundings again, Clint caught sight of another face that was still trying to get a look at him from just inside one of the tents.

That face belonged to Katrina Nolen and when she saw Clint look straight at her, she turned and quickly moved back into the tent. Clint took off after her, finding that folks around him were just as quick to step out of his way as they'd been to clear a path for Hackett's guards.

TWENTY-ONE

The time for sneaking around and following from a distance was over. Clint might have preferred to pick a better time to make his presence in Mescall known, but now he had to deal with the situation left to him. Of course, not having to be subtle any longer did have its advantages.

Clint rushed into the tent and pushed past the dirty cowboys, miners, fighters, and drunks that seemed to fill Mescall the way water filled a bucket. Although the tent was large enough to be sectioned off into a few areas by folding screens, Clint could see enough to pick out Katrina without too much problem.

She was the only blonde in there who was trying desperately to find another way out of that tent.

"Not so fast, Katrina," Clint said as he came up behind her and grabbed hold of her wrist.

Immediately, Katrina turned and let out a pained whine. "Stop it! You're hurting me!"

Clint looked around to see if anyone was buying what she was selling. Although Katrina had drawn a few glances in her direction, even the drunks could tell that Clint wasn't holding onto her tight enough to hurt her. The men that

86

were looking over at them merely nodded and went about their business.

Reaching down, Clint picked Katrina up from where she'd started to collapse onto the floor.

"Nobody's watching," he said. "Don't bother with the act."

"It's not an act," she groaned. "You're hurting me."

"I've barely got ahold of you. Now just quiet down so we can have ourselves a little chat."

Katrina looked around and saw that Clint was right. Rather than let loose the scream she'd been building up, she expelled her breath in a frustrated sigh. "Fine," she said while snatching her arm away from him. "What do you want from me?"

"First of all, I'd like my gun back."

"I don't have it."

"What?"

"You heard me. I don't have your gun. I don't even know what you're talking about."

Although Clint didn't raise a hand to her, Katrina recoiled as though she'd been slapped across the face. Even that wasn't enough to draw any sympathy from the other inhabitants of the tent.

Clint looked down at her without saying a word. In a way, it was gratifying to see her squirm after all the work he'd done to get there. Looking into her eyes at that moment was also enough for Clint to see the guilt written upon her soul.

"I know you took my gun, Katrina. Is that even your real name, or should I find Warren and make him tell me what it is?"

"Katrina's my name," she said as she huffed to a nearby stool and sat down. "And, yes, Warren is truly my brother."

Now that his blood had had a chance to cool, Clint looked around the tent. There were several cots set up in rooms sectioned off by screens or curtains. It reminded him of a few Army field hospitals he'd seen, only with a considerably more festive atmosphere.

Apparently, the tent was one of Mescall's hotels. The air was thick with the smell of too many bodies being forced too close together, and bits of dozens of conversations buzzed around Clint's head. He found another stool within arm's reach and pulled it so he could sit directly in front of Katrina.

"Why steal my gun, Katrina?" he asked. "What did you do with it?"

Well past the point of lying about what she'd done, Katrina sighed and said, "I didn't intend on stealing it. Not at the start. I wanted to meet you." Smiling and batting her eyes, she reached out to run her fingers along Clint's forearm. "You know, just like I told you that night."

"You told me plenty," Clint said while taking Katrina's hand off him. "Now tell me the truth."

"My brother heard about where I was going and he started babbling on about who you were and how famous you are," she said in a rush. "He started crying about how much money he lost at cards and how him and his wife were probably going to lose some of their land or maybe even their house."

She looked at Clint just then with true compassion in her eyes. It was as unmistakable to him as the deceit had been moments ago.

"He was crying," she repeated earnestly. "I never saw my brother cry before. He asked me to steal your gun so he could pay back what he owed."

"Did he tell you I wasn't even the one who won all the money at that game?"

"He didn't have to. I saw enough to know that Nate the Louse walked away with the fattest pockets. It was that little weasel who put this whole notion into my brother's head. The Louse said that if Warren would get your gun and hand it over, he'd pay for it with the money he won."

"Is that all?"

She nodded and reached up to quickly brush away a tear that had formed in the corner of her eye.

"Do you even know how I found you?" Clint asked. "Or how I knew you'd be here?"

"I've heard plenty about you," she said. "And from what I've seen, a lot of it is true. Should I be surprised that you found me?"

Clint studied her face and could tell right away that she wasn't lying. At this point, there was no reason for her not to own up to the note that had been left in her room back in Carte Nueves. At least, there wouldn't be if she knew about it.

"All right, then. Give me my gun and I won't have to take up any more of your time."

"I don't have it," she said as panic rose up in her voice. "I swear. Warren took it from me and—"

"Where's Warren?" Clint asked.

"He's around here somewhere, probably lining up to bet on tonight's fights."

Clint looked around the section of the tent and saw small lockboxes lined up in a row right along with the cots. "Where's his things?"

"We're not staying in here. I just . . . came in here to get away from you."

"That's a lie. Tell me where the cot is that Warren rented."

She squirmed and seemed about to unleash another scream, but most everyone else in the tent had lost interest in her. Judging by what was going on in there, the only thing someone might have done if she did scream was stand by and watch the show.

"It's right over there," she said, nodding toward an empty pair of cots. "But it's not in there."

Taking hold of Katrina's arm in a firm grip, Clint got up and started heading for the cots. She came along with him without much fuss.

"Open it," he said once he got to the cots.

She did, and fidgeted as Clint rooted through their belongings.

"Your gun's not here, Clint, I swear. Warren never let it leave his sight."

"Then you won't be leaving my sight," Clint said as he pulled her toward the door. "Not until I get my gun back."

TWENTY-TWO

By this time, Clint had memorized the simplistic map he'd bought and knew as much as he could about Mescall's setup. Once he'd gotten used to the chaotic jumble of tents and constant flow of swaggering people, it wasn't too difficult to see the method behind Mescall's madness.

He started off dragging Katrina with him toward the section of camp devoted to the fights, and quickly found himself pulled into a whole new layer of chaos. The people were so thick that they practically choked every walkway. The tents themselves were hard to make out until Clint was just about pushed into one.

Even with all that, however, finding the spots where bets were being taken was as hard as finding the bottom of a hill. All Clint had to do was brace himself and follow the natural momentum.

Bets were being accepted by several men standing on their own, but most of the action was being handled by men in booths that were marked by the brand of an H within a circle. Those were probably the men that Hackett, himself, endorsed since they were the ones getting the most play. Also, they were the ones that weren't getting run off by large men carrying shotguns.

"Where's Warren?" Clint asked once he'd taken Katrina to the middle of the gambling district.

She looked around and shook her head. "I don't know. Somewhere around here. But I don't think he's got your gun with him."

"Yeah? And why should I believe you?"

"I don't know. He carries a gun, but not yours. I haven't seen him with it since we got here."

"And why did you come here?"

"Why does anyone come here? For the fights. Warren never misses them. He usually walks away with a profit in winnings. Lord, I hope he makes a profit or we're in some serious trouble."

Clint was getting more and more aggravated with the whole situation. The more time he spent in Mescall, the more he started to think that his gun was being shipped off to God knew where else for God knew what reason.

Just when he was starting to consider the possibility of forgetting the whole deal and crafting a new gun, a familiar voice boomed from a platform set up not too far away.

"I see all you fellas are laying your money down for the night's events," Hackett said through a cone of hardened leather that caused his voice to echo throughout much of the camp. "Since the preliminary bouts are well under way, you all should know that the main events are right on track to start tomorrow night!"

That was met with a round of applause and a good amount of gruff cheers.

Hackett stood on the platform, which put him about four feet higher than the rest of the crowd. There were so many people gathered around him that Clint couldn't see the platform or even most of the lower half of Hackett's body.

"As you all know, I do my damnedest to make sure you folks get the most for your money," Hackett continued. "There's plenty of liquor."

More cheers and applause.

"And enough women to put a smile on yer faces no matter what!"

The cheers degenerated into catcalls as well as a few howls.

Next to Clint, Katrina yelped and jumped a bit as an overly eager hand swatted her on the backside. She pulled her wrist out of Clint's grasp so she could wrap both arms around him instead.

The only one who could calm the crowd was Hackett, and he did so by patting the air and waving his hands until it was quiet enough for his voice to be heard. "Now, I know there's plenty of you out there who have more than a passing interest in these fights. There's over fifty men signed up to fight. There's managers, families, trainers, and plenty more that will surely join in once things get under way.

"How do I know that? Well, let me just say that I wouldn't be surprised if the number of fights on the schedule doubles once you get a look at what you all will be fighting for."

With that, three of Hackett's guards stepped onto the platform. One of them carried a dented lockbox that was similar to the ones in the sleeping tent. The other two flanked him brandishing the shotguns common among Hackett's men.

"Of course, there's the prize money, which will be more than ten thousand dollars to the winner."

Cheers. Applause.

"But the truly special item is this year's Grand Prize!"

The crowd actually quieted down as everyone leaned in to see what would come out of that box.

Clint was getting a bad feeling in the pit of his stomach.

Hackett waited for nearly a solid minute before reaching out to open the box. Even as he fit a key into the lock, he took his time until it seemed the crowd was close to charging the platform, armed guards or not. Finally, Hackett flung open the box and reached inside.

"Gentlemen," Hackett bellowed. "I present to you an item that is not only rare, but has historical significance. An item that cannot even be given a dollar value. But let me assure you that there isn't another like it in the world. It's a prize that will be wanted by museums. A prize you can pass down for generations to come. A prize that has been sought after by some of the most notorious gunfighters in recent memory!"

"Oh, no," Clint said under his breath as the knot in his stomach was cinched in a little tighter.

"I present to you the pistol of Clint Adams himself!" Hackett said while lifting his hand over his head to show the very thing Clint had ridden all this way to see. "The weapon of The Gunsmith!"

Clint's jaw dropped as a round of applause and cheers went up through the crowd of drunks and gamblers.

Katrina dug her elbow into Clint's ribs just enough to get his attention when she muttered, "See, I told you my brother didn't have that thing."

TWENTY-THREE

Clint didn't let Hackett out of his sight. He also didn't take his eyes off the guards who were watching over his gun as if it was made out of solid gold. The gun, itself, was easiest to spot. It was being waved about and shown around more than a prize hog at a county fair.

Men lined up to get a look at it and Hackett spoke to them all. From the looks on their faces and the animated discussions that were being held, it was obvious that Hackett's feet were being dragged over the coals by every man who crossed his path.

"Good," Clint said to himself with a smirk. "I hope trying to prove that's the genuine article is more trouble than it's worth."

And before Clint could get too pleased with himself, he saw one of the guards tap Hackett on the shoulder and then point straight to him. Hackett took a moment to squint through the crowd before fixing his eyes on Clint and tossing him a friendly wave.

When Clint felt a tap on his own shoulder, he almost jumped out of his skin.

"Whoa, there," Rick Hartman said. "I know I'm a little

late, but there's no need to get that upset. It's only about a quarter past seven."

Clint let out the breath that had jumped into his throat, and then realized that he'd drawn his gun halfway from his holster out of reflex. Dropping the weapon back into place, he gave Hartman an apologetic shrug.

"Sorry about that," Clint said. "You startled me."

"First time anyone's been able to do that in a while," Hartman said.

"In a crowd like this, it's not all that hard. I'm only human."

"Not if you listen to the stories I've heard. By the way, I found Nate."

"And I found my gun," Clint said sarcastically. "Turns out I had the easiest job."

"Really? How so?"

Clint turned and looked at Hartman head-on. He could tell his old friend wasn't pulling his leg. "You haven't heard?"

Hartman shook his head. "It's hard to hear much of anything when you're elbow to elbow with about a thousand of my new best friends. I did hear the fights were delayed for some big announcement."

Clint filled him in on what that announcement was and finished by nodding toward Hackett's platform. "Go on up there and take a look for yourself."

"Me? I thought you would've been up there already to reclaim your property."

"I will, but first I'd like to hear what he's saying to all those men up there. Just get in line and listen to the pitch."

The first fight was about to start and the crowd outside was actually thinning out. Hartman walked up to the platform and waited for a few minutes before one of the guards motioned for him to go up and take a look at what Hackett was displaying.

Clint hung back and watched. While he'd been anxious

to go up there and take what was his, he found it more interesting to see the looks on the faces of the men who did go up there. It seemed that Hackett wasn't having an easy time of it.

"You going to take on all those men?" came a voice from beside Clint.

Glancing over, Clint was a little surprised to find Katrina still standing where he'd left her. "You can go," he said. "I'm not the sort to keep hostages."

"I'm no hostage," she said defiantly. "And even if I was, I'd be safer with you than in the middle of these animals."

"You are a thief, though. Leave. Now."

"I told you why I took that gun," she huffed. "And I helped you find it."

"That's why I'm letting you go. What more do you want from me?"

For a moment, Katrina didn't say anything. She looked around with a lost expression in her eyes as if she'd been abandoned in the middle of an open stretch of trail. Looking back to Clint, she pulled herself up and faced him. "My brother's no thief, either. He's a good man who got in over his head. There are plenty like him around here. You want to see for yourself, just go to those fights and you'll see plenty."

"You told me your brother was here to gamble."

"And as you saw for yourself, he's not too good at that."

"If your brother needs help, he should find a better way to go about asking for it. A good place to start is doing some talking for himself."

She took Clint's hand and moved up close to him. "Please, Clint. I'm asking for your help. Just let me and my brother have some of your time and we can explain."

Clint looked down into her eyes and felt a reaction deep inside him. There was genuine emotion there, which not even the best bluffer could fake. Placing a finger under her chin, Clint said, "I trusted my instincts where you were concerned once already and it didn't turn out too good. You'll have to do a little more than bat your eyelashes at me to get me to do it again."

Although he didn't push her away, Clint turned away from her just enough to get his point across. He felt Katrina's hand linger on his shoulder. Then, it drifted across his back as she walked away.

Then, she was gone.

Before Clint could think too much about her, he saw Hartman making his way back toward him from the platform.

"It's your gun, all right," Hartman said. "But I don't think everyone believes it."

"That's what it looked like from here."

"I can tell you one thing, though. Hackett does a hell of a job convincing folks. From what I heard, half the people that left that platform were convinced. And something else I can tell you is that he won't be giving up that gun to anyone but the winner of his main event."

Clint thought that over for a moment, shook his head, and started walking toward the large tent where everyone else had been going.

"Where are you off to?" Hartman asked.

"My gun's here. It's in safe hands and it's not going anywhere. It's been a long day. Let's go watch the fights."

Hartman smirked and nodded. After catching up to Clint, he said, "Let's stop off at the betting window. Maybe I can win enough to buy the damn gun back."

TWENTY-FOUR

It was the biggest tent in camp and was about the same size as a small saloon. Propped up by a series of poles that worked their way around the perimeter, it was supported in the middle by a wooden frame similar to the rafters in a normal roof. When Clint walked through the wobbling frame of the wide door, he expected to feel cramped and confined since the tent wasn't much more than eight or nine feet tall.

The inside of the tent, however, was a whole other story. It was also a pleasant surprise for both Clint and Hartman, who'd spent too much time elbow to elbow with grimy drunks. Only the edge of the inner area was at normal ground level. From there, it dropped down like a series of steps that made their way into the very bottom, which was a good twenty feet down.

The smell of freshly turned soil filled the tent, which was a hell of an improvement considering the stench that pervaded most of the camp. Taking a quick look around, Clint was reminded of a coliseum from the old days of Rome. The steps heading down to the bottom were filling up with people sitting down and hanging their legs off the front. A few rows were kept empty so people could climb

99

up or down, giving the pit more order than anything else in Mescall.

Most of the space for seating was already filled and guards had taken up their spots around the upper edge. The bottom of the pit was a rough circle about ten feet in diameter. The sides were reinforced with wooden planks and the floor was left as packed soil.

"Hell of a setup," Hartman said.

The noise inside the place would have been plenty loud under normal circumstances. With the noise being contained inside a pit with a canvas roof over it, Clint was barely able to hear himself think.

"Huh?" Clint asked, leaning in toward Hartman.

"I said it's a hell of a setup!"

"Oh. Yeah, it is!" Clint shouted, knowing that his voice could just barely make it over the rest of the noise. "Where should we sit?"

"Huh?"

Just as Clint was pulling in a breath so he could scream in Hartman's ear, he felt a hand clap down on his shoulder. The owner of that hand was one of Hackett's towering guards.

The big man with the shotgun leaned down and spoke in a rumbling tone that was just loud enough for both other men to hear. "Mr. Hackett has saved you some good seats. Right down there, second row from the bottom."

Clint had already spotted Hackett making his way into the tent. When Clint looked over at him, he got a nod and wave from the barrel-chested man.

"You can place bets from your seat in the bottom two rows," the guard explained.

That seemed to have answered the question in Hartman's mind and the bartender slapped his hands together anxiously. "All right," he said. "Let's get down there before we lose those seats. Some men would sell their sisters to get those seats."

"What?" Clint shouted.

"I said let's go!"

Rather than look a gift horse in the mouth, Clint followed Hartman down the side of the pit. After a few steps, it became obvious that most of the sides had also been reinforced with boards and covered by canvas. Enough dirt had been kicked up from all the traffic, however, to cover the canvas until it looked like just another hole in the ground.

After several close calls from nearly being knocked into that hole by a clumsy elbow or a stumbling drunk, Clint and Hartman found their spots and sat down. From this closer perspective, Clint could see that there had already been some serious fights recently. The floor of the pit was spattered with dark stains that were a little too red to be water.

Hartman was rubbing his hands together like he was sitting down to a Thanksgiving Day feast. His eyes bounced from one spot to another, quickly picking out the muscled brutes who were flexing their arms, cracking their knuckles, and generally playing up to the crowd.

"You see that one there?" Hartman asked. "That fella fought the last time I was here. It was his first go-around and he put on a hell of a show. He's got to be one of the favorites."

"How many of these things did you attend?" Clint asked.

"Just one of these, but there are fights held all the time. They come through Labyrinth or other spots nearby. West Texas is a great spot for professional fights. You'd know that if you weren't out riding all over the country all the time."

Clint felt something batting against his arm. When he turned to get a look, the man sitting in the row above him handed down a stack of papers that were wrinkled and stained enough to have been swept up off the street.

"Great," Hartman said. "There's the program for the fights." He reached across Clint, took a sheet from the pile, and passed the stack on to the closest neighbor he could reach. "There's plenty of names I recognize, here. Plenty of new blood, too. This should be great!"

But Clint wasn't looking at the program. Instead, he was watching as a trim redhead eased into the row and sat down beside him. Her hair hung wild and loose over her shoulders, framing a well-structured face and a set of thick, inviting lips.

"Each fight is five rounds," Hartman explained, still oblivious to the fact that Clint wasn't paying him much attention. "Each round's three or five minutes long. I forget which it is."

"It's five minutes," the redhead said.

Surprised at the smooth, feminine voice, Hartman glanced around and got a look at the redhead. He wasn't too surprised, however, to find the attractive woman sitting next to Clint. "You always find the best in the lot," Hartman said to Clint with a shake of his head.

"What?" Clint asked over the noise.

"Never mind."

TWENTY-FIVE

Clint shrugged and shifted so he could get a better look at the redhead. "Are you another guest of Mr. Hackett's?"

"You might say that." Extending a hand, she shook Clint's and said, "My name's Althea, but I go by Tia."

"Nice to meet you, Tia. I'm Clint."

Her grip was firm and there was no mistaking the interest in her eyes when she looked at Clint. Her smile was subtle, but genuine, curling her lips into a curve almost as seductive as the lines of her figure. Tia wore what appeared to be black men's work pants. Despite the simple cut of the fabric, they rode low on her waist and were unable to keep her rounded hips hidden away.

Her shirt was cut like a man's as well, but tied at the bottom in a way that showed a little hint of her flat stomach. It was unbuttoned halfway, but she did wear a cotton undershirt beneath it that clung to her firm, rounded breasts.

After a lingering smile, Tia shifted so she was looking down into the pit. She pulled her legs up close so her knees were pressed against her chest and she wrapped her arms around them to keep them snug. The expression on her face was that of giddy excitement. In an odd sort of way, it reminded Clint of the occupant of the seat on his other side.

"This is great," Hartman said. "Looks like things are just about to start."

As if on cue, one of the muscled men who'd been perched on the edge of the pit hopped down and landed on the uneven floor. As soon as his boots hit the dirt, he raised both arms over his head and let out a bellowing roar for the crowd.

The unruly spectators responded in kind and kept their enthusiasm going until the fighter's opponent dropped into the pit as well.

Both men were thick with muscle and covered in scars. Their faces were gnarled and leathery and there wasn't one normal-looking ear between them.

"Those fellas look like they've been chewed up and spit out," Clint said.

"Yeah," Tia replied. "I love these fights."

Hartman laughed, but didn't take his eyes from the fighters.

"You've been to many of these?" Clint asked.

She nodded enthusiastically.

Below, the fighters squared off and tossed a few choice insults back and forth.

"Our first bout this evening," Hackett announced from his spot in the crowd, "is between Randall and Iverson."

Each of the fighters raised his arms at the sound of his name, each of them getting an equal amount of applause and boos.

"Fight!"

With that command from Hackett, each of the fighters bared his teeth and threw himself at his opponent. Although both of them were hulking beasts, Iverson was slightly bigger. Randall, on the other hand, was a little quicker on his feet.

"My money's on Randall," Tia said from beside Clint. "What about you?"

"I didn't get a chance to bet."

"Iverson," Hartman said.

Clint looked over to Hartman and asked, "When did you place a bet?"

"While you were making eyes at the ladies." To confirm his story, Hartman held up a little stub of torn paper for Clint to see. Sure enough, there was "Iverson—two dollers" scrawled upon the paper.

"Your friend there is in the spirit of things," Tia said.

Suddenly, the crowd erupted into an explosion of shouts and bellows as the slightly bigger Iverson reared back and landed a powerful right hook on Randall's jaw. Blood sprayed from the lankier man's mouth and a tooth flew through the air. After spitting out a wad of red saliva, Randall ducked under a second swing and charged forward with both arms held open.

Tia winced and shook her head. "Oh, now that's a mistake. You just watch."

Randall got his arms around Iverson's midsection and started pummeling the bigger man's ribs. Once Iverson steeled himself, he balled his fists and raised one of them over his head. Instead of punching Randall, he dropped his elbow straight down onto his back.

That brought half the crowd to its feet, including Rick Hartman.

Tia was already shaking her head and ripping her ticket in half. "Can't win them all," she said.

Randall did his damnedest to get away from the bigger man, but soon caught another elbow in the kidney, which dropped him to the ground.

Iverson used his foot to roll Randall onto his back before standing over him and reaching down to take hold of him by his hair. He paused just long enough to play up to the crowd before delivering one last punch straight into Randall's face.

When that last fist struck, it could be heard throughout the entire pit. Bone crunched against bone, driving one ragged breath out of Randall that had been pulled up from his toes.

There wasn't a man in that arena who couldn't see the light flicker out of Randall's eyes like a candle that had been blown out. When Iverson let go of Randall's head, the smaller man's chin hit the floor. Randall instinctively tried to get back up again, but everyone knew it was over.

"We have a winner!" Hackett shouted.

Hartman jumped to his feet and let out a victorious shout, right along with everyone else who had backed the bigger of the two fighters. From there, the place exploded with cheers as the fighters were helped up out of the pit. One of them, of course, needed a little more help than the other.

Clint felt his blood pump quicker through his veins as the spirit of the fight seeped into him. Having Tia's tight little body so close to him wasn't hurting things, either. "Who's your next pick?" he asked.

"I always put my money on speed over power. In this next fight, I suggest you do the same." With that, she leaned over and kissed Clint on the lips before jumping to her feet and making her way to the bottom of the pit.

TWENTY-SIX

Clint was on his feet and about to jump down after her when he heard Hackett's voice booming through the arena.

"Fight number two on tonight's schedule . . . Avery and Werner!"

Hartman put a hand on Clint's shoulder and pushed him back into his seat. "Hold on there, friend. Looks like the lady knows what she's doing."

Even though Clint could see Tia strutting in that pit and working the crowd into a lather, he still couldn't believe it. The smile on her face couldn't have been wider. When she spotted him, she pointed him out and gave him a wink.

"Fight!"

Tia's opponent was a young man who looked as confused as Clint had been. He stood just over six feet tall and had a mess of shoulder-length hair that looked more like straw sprouting from his scalp. Werner wore coveralls and worn-out boots, making him look like a farmer that had been pulled right out of the fields.

Werner looked up at Hackett and started to talk, but was silenced when Hackett jabbed a thick finger at him and told him to get to work.

"Do it, boy," Hackett shouted. "Or the deal's off."

Clint could barely make out those words. He might have lost them all amid the cheering and hollering of the crowd, but Hackett's voice was like a plow that cut right through everything else under that canvas roof.

Tia was still dancing around the pit, shaking out her arms and loosening up her neck. When she saw Werner turn to face her and raise his fists, she smiled and hunkered down into a stance of her own.

The blond man's first swing was slow, meant to test and see what she would do. Tia's reaction was quicker than anyone expected as she slapped away the punch as though it was an insult to her sensibilities.

"Come on now," she taunted. "This is supposed to be a fight. You don't want to get showed up by a woman, do you?"

But Werner was still hesitant. Clint could see something going on inside the young man's head. More than likely, it had to do with facing the choice of either hitting a woman to win or suffering public humiliation with a loss.

"All right, then," Tia said loudly enough to be heard by all. "I'll make it easy for you."

With that, she snapped forward with a jab that was almost too quick to see. Her arm flicked out like a bullwhip and her fist connected against the solid muscle of Werner's stomach.

The punch obviously didn't hurt too badly, but it shocked the hell out of the young man on the receiving end. He recoiled a bit and stepped away from her, causing the entire pit to fill up with cheers for Tia and taunts aimed at every aspect of Werner's masculinity.

Feeding off the wild atmosphere, Tia moved forward and around Werner with as much grace as a dancer. She hopped on the balls of her feet while keeping her arms in close to her body. When she got within striking distance, she slowed down just enough for Werner to draw a bead on her.

Werner's hand swung out again, this time with more

force and intent. It was an open-handed strike, however, and didn't come any closer to hitting her than his first swing.

This time, Tia bowed at the waist and pivoted to one side to duck completely under the swing. Even Clint had to admit that he was captivated by the ease of her movements and the skill with which she controlled the fight.

In a fraction of a second, Tia was behind Werner. She twisted herself around and dropped down in a spinning, corkscrew maneuver. After she'd wound herself up, she brought one leg around in another whipping strike that connected at the back of Werner's legs.

Before he knew what was happening, Werner felt his feet come right out from under him. His arms flailed wildly and he hit the ground hard on his back. Even from where Clint was sitting, he could hear some of the wind get knocked out of the man's lungs.

The look on Werner's face was shifting from uncertainty to anger. Now that he'd taken a few hits, he was losing his apprehension about fighting a woman. It seemed that that was just fine with Tia.

Wearing an excited grin, she rolled onto her side while snapping her foot out in a quick, downward kick aimed at Werner's midsection. The kick was deflected at the last possible moment by the man's forearm. Although it wasn't pretty, it worked well enough to keep him from getting hit again.

"That's more like it," Tia said. "Now are you ready to give these folks the fight they paid to see?"

After scooting back, Werner got to his feet and looked up at Hackett once more. He saw something in those eyes that lit a fire under him. When he looked back to Tia, he lifted his arms and balled his calloused hands into fists.

TWENTY-SEVEN

Werner lashed out with a series of punches. They weren't nearly as quick as Tia's kick, but anyone could see there was a whole lot more power behind them. One of his fists cut through empty air as Tia jumped to one side to avoid it. The other fist connected, clipping her chin and sending her sprawling back.

Although she staggered a bit, Tia kept on her feet. She made sure to back away until her shoulder bumped against the side of the pit, where she reached up and rubbed her jaw. The tip of her tongue flicked out to run against her bottom lip. There wasn't any blood there, but she nodded as if to give Werner credit for the hit anyway.

"That all you got?" Tia asked with a challenging smirk. "I guess this is what it feels like to fight a woman."

That hit Werner with more of an impact than anything else so far. She'd tossed the insult out there for everyone to hear and the crowd ate it up like candy.

Werner was a young man, with a young man's pride. Hearing those words from Tia just then was the equivalent of having that pride stripped down and slapped around for all to see. To make matters worse, Tia was charging straight at him without an ounce of fear in her eyes.

She ran up and ducked to one side while stiff-arming Werner in the gut. Her forearm bounced off him. The only effect it seemed to have was to make the fire in his belly burn even hotter.

When Tia came around to kick him below the belt, Werner shoved her with both hands and sent her reeling away from him. Since she wasn't going to stop coming at him, he did the only thing he could and started taking the offensive.

Werner swung at her again and again. Each time, his fists caught no more than a piece of their intended target. Many times, they caught nothing but empty air.

"He's gonna take her head off," Hartman said to Clint.

Clint shook his head. "He's holding back. I don't think he could even get ahold of her if he went full out."

"Seems like she might have a chance, then."

"A chance? This fight could have been over long ago."

"What?" Hartman asked without taking his eyes from the spectacle in the pit. "How do you figure?"

"She's holding back, too."

Now that she'd caught a few punches and was really working to avoid Werner's swings, Tia seemed to be focused. The smile never left her face and her movements only got more complex as the fight went on. Finally, she came to a stop with her back a pace or two away from the wall.

Tia hopped forward, ducked low, and snapped both hands out to catch Werner just under the ribs. She stayed put just long enough to let him commit himself to a follow-up punch, and then straightened up to her full height.

Werner gritted his teeth and swung with a lunging punch intended to put her down for good. One moment, his fist had been speeding toward Tia's face. The next moment, she was gone and his knuckles were headed straight for one of the wooden panels reinforcing the inner wall of the pit.

The punch landed with a solid thump that rattled the entire pit as well as everyone sitting alongside it. Clint swore he felt the impact through the ground beneath him. Judging by the uproar in the crowd, he wasn't the only one.

Werner's knuckles slammed against wood and packed earth. Dust bellowed out from behind the board and trickled down onto the ground. He stood there with his arm extended as though his fist his been embedded into the side of the pit.

Tia was standing directly beside him, crouched and ready for her opponent's next move.

But there was no move coming.

Werner peeled his hand back, leaving a good amount of blood and skin on the wall. The expression on his face was of open-mouthed surprise. His eyes widened at the sight of his bloody hand. They widened even further when they spotted Tia standing so close to him, looking on with interest.

First, a stunned groan had rippled through the crowd. Then, directly following the missed punch, there was another wave of cheers. That last sound was something that Tia had been waiting for, and she kept it going by tossing a flirtatious smile up into the seats.

Just as Werner was about to suck up another breath and come at her again, he lost sight of Tia as she raced around behind him. This time, she didn't punch or kick him, but hopped up onto his back and locked her arms around his neck.

Leaning in close, she whispered something into Werner's ear. As she kept talking, Tia cinched her grip tighter around Werner's throat.

In a matter of seconds, the man in coveralls dropped to one knee. His face was red as a beet and his arms were reaching out to grab at nothing but open air.

Tia hung onto him like a tick. Her head was in tight against Werner's ear, making it impossible for the man to crack skulls with her. She hung on as Werner dropped to both knees, and even hung on as he crumpled over to the dirt.

Everyone under that canvas tent held their breath.

Even Hackett was leaning forward to get a look at what would happen next.

Clint watched Tia ease up on her grip just enough so she could get a good look at the man in her grasp.

Hartman clutched the ticket in his hand, silently mouthing his words of encouragement to the name scrawled upon the slip.

Finally, Tia let Werner go.

She loosened her arms from his neck and rolled away to leave the muscled young man where he lay. Getting to her feet, she used the tip of her toe to roll him onto his back. From there, Tia placed one foot flat upon his chest and raised both arms into the air.

The crowd let loose with a deafening roar and everyone jumped to their feet.

TWENTY-EIGHT

"Just when I thought I'd seen it all," Hartman said after hollering right along with everyone else, "someone like that comes along."

Clint was clapping as well, admiring Tia's form as she took her bows. "I've got to admit, she's impressive."

"Impressive as hell, but part of me wishes that Werner would've had a little more grit in his system."

"What part is that?"

"The part that made me buy this ticket." As he said that, Hartman held up the slip that he'd been holding for Clint to see.

Once again, Hartman had managed to place a bet without Clint even seeing him do it. And, once again, Hartman had put his money down on the wrong person to win the fight.

"You bet on Werner?"

"Sure," Hartman said in his own defense. "He was the one that Hackett mentioned back at his wagon, right?"

Clint straightened up and reflexively looked back at Hackett. "Yeah. I almost forgot about that."

"Well, I didn't. The fight might be fixed, but that's no reason for me not to make a little money off of it. And don't even give me the speech, Clint. I already know what you're going to say."

"Is that so? Then maybe you should tell me, because the fight obviously wasn't fixed the way you thought it was."

Hartman's brow furrowed as he looked back and forth between Tia and Werner in the pit and Hackett perched outside it. "Good point. But he did say something about Werner in the second."

Shrugging, Clint said, "Well, this was the second fight of the night and Werner was in it. Maybe that's all it was."

The more Hartman thought about that, the less he liked it. "That's all he was talking about? The schedule? Wait a second." With that, he found the schedule he'd been handed at the beginning of the night and scanned the list of names.

"I'll be damned," Hartman groaned. "The next fight has a fighter named Dilkins and the one after that has an Offermann." Hartman crumpled the schedule into a ball and tossed it. "So much for that plan." Suddenly, he snapped his fingers and brightened up. "Wait a second! Maybe those are the names of the ones that are supposed to lose!"

Clint patted his friend on the shoulder and got up. "I'll leave you to make the big plan. I've got somewhere else to be."

"Somewhere else? What do you mean by that? There is nothing else!" Although Clint was already up and walking away, Hartman kept right on shouting at him. "This is why we're here. This is why everyone's here!"

But Clint wasn't paying him any mind. At least, no more mind than it took for him to toss a wave over his shoulder as he headed down toward the bottommost row of seats.

In the pit, Werner was back up and trying to get to his feet. Although his steps were a little shaky and his face was still red, he seemed to be pulling himself together well enough. He recoiled for a moment when Tia came bounding up to him, but quickly saw the smile on her face.

Speaking low enough to keep her words between herself and Werner, Tia shook his hand and patted him on the cheek. When she left him, the man in coveralls couldn't help but smile right back at her.

Clint was walking toward the edge of the pit and Tia was rushing over to meet him. The energy in her steps could be felt in the air and the twitch in her hips was a sight to behold.

Hartman's mind was churning away at what his next bet would be. By this point, the man who took the bets for that section came over to Hartman's side without having to be beckoned in the slightest. The man was about half the size of a normal man and was built perfectly to maneuver through the teeming crowd of the arena.

"What'll it be, mister?" the little man asked.

By then, Clint was leaning down to extend a hand to where Tia was watching him with seductive, hungry eyes. The moment he was in reach, she leapt up and wrapped her arms around his neck in an embrace that almost pulled Clint straight down onto the bottom floor.

"Jesus Christ," Hartman said while shaking his head. "If only I could put money down on what he'll be doing tonight."

"Come on, mister, I ain't got all night."

Hartman dropped back down into his seat and dug some money out of his pocket. "Who's fighting Dilkins?"

"That'd be Conway."

"Here," Hartman said while handing over his cash. "Put this on Conway."

By the time Hartman had his newest slip in hand, Clint was nowhere to be found.

TWENTY-NINE

"Now that was a hell of a fight," Clint said once he'd finally stopped moving.

After meeting up with Tia, he'd been swept away by the redhead, who still moved like the whirlwind she'd been in her fight. Tia didn't need a bit of help coming out of the pit and practically made it into Clint's arms with one jump.

Taking his hand in hers, she'd led the way through the crowd and out a side door leading from the arena. It happened so quickly that Clint barely even realized he was outside until the cheers built up to another roar and Hackett announced the next set of fighters.

Tia's expression was pure excitement. Her eyes flashed with a light all their own as she reached out to take Clint's face in her hands and press her mouth against his in a fiery kiss.

Her lips were soft and hot, as was the rest of her body, which was pressed up against Clint's. She'd worked up a bit of a sweat in her fight, but just enough to get her heart racing. As Clint wrapped his arms around her and pressed her against the closest wall he could find, her heart pounded against him like a series of quick jabs.

Every woman had a distinct taste and smell. Tia's was

spicy, through and through. Her tight body writhed against him eagerly and her mouth opened to allow her tongue to flick out against Clint's lips. When Clint slid his fingers through her thick red hair, he could hear and feel Tia's moan as it worked its way up into her throat.

"What did you say?" she asked breathlessly.

It took Clint a moment to remember what he had just said. With the heat of their kiss still working its way down his body, it was getting difficult for him to focus on anything else.

"Oh, I said that was a hell of a fight."

When she smiled, the corners of her mouth curled up and then she crinkled her eyes. "Thanks. I think that boy was fresh off a farm. Sometimes, fellas will think that winning a few saloon brawls makes them tough enough to make it in Mescall."

"You talk like a real professional."

"That's because I am," she replied while sliding her fingers up and down Clint's stomach. "You didn't strike me as the type who would make the mistake of underestimating me."

Clint pressed his hands flat against her sides and worked them all the way down her body. He could feel the roundness of her hips and kept his hands there as she squirmed back and forth in his grasp. "I'd say surprised was more like it," he said.

Balancing on one foot, Tia wrapped one leg around Clint and rubbed it up and down against him. She got him in a grip tight enough for him to feel the muscles in her thigh turn to steely strips beneath her flesh as she pulled him tight against her body.

"You never seen a woman fight?" she asked.

"Not like you fought."

"I did get a little lucky in there. I think it was because of that kiss before I went in."

Clint had forgotten about the rest of the world just then.

With Tia wrapped around him and wriggling in all the right places, he didn't mind letting everything else go for a little while longer.

Then again, he suddenly remembered what had happened the last time he'd let himself be so comfortable with a woman.

Despite what was going through Clint's mind, it was Tia who broke away first. Her leg relaxed from where it had been wrapped around him, but her arms remained draped over his shoulders.

"You're staying for the rest of the fights, aren't you?" she asked in a way that was more of a request.

"Yeah. I'll be here for a while."

"Good. I've got another fight and I'd hate to see my good-luck charm pick up and leave."

"Good-luck charm? I thought that certain things weren't good for someone before they get into a fight."

She smirked and ran her tongue along the side of Clint's neck. "I've heard that, too. Mostly from boxers."

Tia's breath was hot against his skin and her hips writhed against the erection growing between his legs.

Looking around, Clint took in his surroundings to see how far he needed to go in order to be alone with her. They were standing outside the main tent, leaning against a wagon parked nearby. It wasn't the same wagon Clint had approached before, but was about the same size as Hackett's.

The only people in sight were several yards away and were either on their way into the main tent or heading in the opposite direction to where the liquor was being served. The sun was long gone, leaving only the stars and a few sputtering torches to illuminate the night.

In the short time Clint had taken to have his look around, Tia hadn't stopped moving her hands and body in a slow grinding rhythm that was driving them both to distraction. Giving in to what they both wanted, Clint reached

down and cupped her backside in his hands. Tia jumped up
and wrapped her legs around him with ease.

Moving away from the noise of the main tent, Clint
walked around the wagon with Tia in his hands. Fortu-
nately, the wagon was not only empty, but also on the edge
of what little torchlight there was in camp.

Once they were enveloped in shadow, Clint backed her
against the wagon. As he moved in closer so he was between her legs, Clint felt Tia's hands busily tugging apart
his belt and loosening his pants. She stood on her feet just
long enough to wriggle out of her own clothes so she was
naked from the waist down.

"You'd better not try to take advantage, Clint," she
teased. "I can handle myself pretty well."

Clint lifted her up again and felt his penis slide against
the warm, moist lips between her thighs. "Actually, I was
going to see how well I could handle you."

As Clint slid inside her, Tia leaned back against the
wagon and let out a slow, satisfied breath.

THIRTY

Her body was solid and muscular, yet light in Clint's arms. He could feel the tight curves of her figure and feel the way she moved in time to his rhythm even though she was being held up off the ground. When Clint found a spot that hit her just right, she arched her back and pumped her hips to make it even better.

Clint massaged her tight, rounded buttocks as he thrust in and out of her. Every inch of her was heated from the fight she'd been in, yet she still had more than enough energy to make his knees tremble.

Every time she kissed him, it was hard and passionate. Their hands moved over each other with urgency, and he found himself plunging into her with more power every time he pumped his hips forward. Soon, Tia was digging her fingernails into Clint's shoulders and pressing her head against the wagon.

Her legs spread open and she let Clint pump his hips to his own rhythm. A few more seconds of that was enough to get her body shaking and soon, Clint had to support her a little more to keep her off the ground. When he felt her climax, Clint pushed all the way inside her and held himself there.

Her pussy clenched around him as the orgasm swept through her body. When it passed, she opened her eyes and looked at him with a new sort of longing. This time, she smiled hungrily and started grinding her hips in little circles.

"You like that?" she asked. One hand was still wrapped around the back of Clint's neck while the other reached up to push against the wagon.

Clint looked down at the lines of her body. The moonlight brushed against the rough texture of her shirt, which made a stark contrast to the smoother contours of her stomach and groin. Her abdomen was a supple curve of muscle, but still remained very feminine. When she worked her hips to take Clint in and out of her, those muscles tensed and stretched to the rhythm of her movements.

Opening her legs a bit allowed her to take his cock all the way inside her. She then pushed her legs together as much as she could while keeping him between them. Clint felt her grow tighter around him, easing his rigid cock in and out of her an inch or two at a time.

The muscles in her stomach tightened again as she started pumping her hips back and forth. Although the motion was something of an imitation of what Clint had been doing earlier, it felt a whole lot different from where he was standing.

She arched her back and gritted her teeth, doing her best not to make enough noise to attract any unwanted attention. The muscles in her legs were like strips of iron and held onto Clint in a way that made it clear she wasn't about to let him go.

Holding onto Tia's hips, Clint drank in the sight of her as she pumped her hips and fought back the urge to scream out as her body started to tremble. Her buttocks fit perfectly into his cupped hands as he moved them up and down along the lower half of her body.

Clint didn't even have to move anymore. All he did was

support her weight as she glided back and forth along the length of his cock. Her stomach glistened with sweat, which dripped in tiny rivulets along the contours of her smoothly sculpted muscle. Reaching up with one hand, Clint massaged her breasts and found them even fuller than he'd expected.

The clothes Tia wore were tough and served a purpose. That purpose was not to make her look attractive, but there was honestly no way for her to look ugly. The thick cotton layers were more like wrapping on a present and Clint was very surprised by just how good that present was.

Her breasts were firm and plump, topped with small nipples, which were now fully erect. Tia let out a little moan when Clint rolled his fingers over her nipple. She then immediately looked around to make sure nobody had heard her.

There wasn't anyone standing nearby that they could see. The only sounds they could hear were the roars coming from the main tent as the next fight moved along.

That little pause in their motions was enough to make the sensations even more intense when they started up again. Both Clint and Tia were conscious of their surroundings. Both of them knew full well that they could be discovered at any time.

Although they weren't exactly trying to hide from anyone in particular, that notion made what they were doing even more exciting.

Clint looked down and took in the sight of their joined bodies with fresh eyes. Tia's shirt had been pulled open and partially draped over her stomach. Her large, rounded breasts were framed nicely in the open flaps of her shirt, and one of them was bare for Clint to see.

She was looking down as well, sliding one hand along the front of her own body while admiring the sight of Clint's. Her fingers traced a line that started at the base of her neck, went between her breasts, and continued all the way to the thatch of hair between her legs.

Once her fingers found her clitoris, she clenched her eyes shut and started bucking against Clint with renewed passion. Her hand made small circles around her sensitive flesh while also grazing along Clint's penis as it slid in and out of her.

Clint had felt a renewed flush of energy as well. His grip tightened on her hips and buttocks as he pulled her toward him, again and again, in time to her movements. Feeling the way her pussy clenched around him, combined with the light touch of her fingers, was enough to drive Clint out of his mind. He could feel the pleasure building up inside him and wasn't inclined to hold it back.

Tia was about to explode as well and struggled more and more to keep her moans to herself.

"Miss Avery!"

Hearing that caused both Clint and Tia to freeze.

"Miss Avery, are you here?"

The voice was coming from nearby and belonged to Nate DeLouse.

Clint and Tia looked at each other with smiles that would have been more at home on the faces of kids in their teens caught rolling around in a loft. Although Clint moved forward to whisper that they should get dressed, that motion in itself was enough to push them both closer to their climax.

The next few thrusts of Clint's hips came in total silence and sent such intense pleasure through both of them that they almost made more noise than the rest of the camp combined.

THIRTY-ONE

"Miss Avery?" Nate whined as he stumbled from one shadow to another. "Miss Avery? I need to speak to you. Are you here?"

Rather than knock against yet another box or stake that he couldn't see, Nate took a moment and planted his feet. Propping his hands upon his hips, he turned at the waist toward every sound that caught his attention. For a man as jittery as Nate DeLouse, nearly every sound in the air fell under that category.

"What was that?" Nate asked as his ears perked up and he tensed at a sound that was a whole lot closer than the others. He knew he'd seen Tia leave this way and didn't think she would miss any more of the fights than it took for her to catch her breath and get some fresh air.

"Miss Avery? Is that you?"

When he felt the hand drop onto his shoulder, Nate damn near jumped out of his skin.

"Of course it's me," she said breathlessly. "Who else would it be?"

"Oh, you scared me."

"A little nervous, are we?"

"Ehhhh, of course not. I was just, ehhh, making sure you got your payment."

Even in the sparse light that came from the moon and the sputtering torches, Tia looked a bit flushed. Most of that came more from the flicker in her eyes and brightness of her smile than the actual color in her face.

Holding out one hand, she gave Nate just enough of a smirk to trip him up as he fumbled in his pockets. "Did you see my fight?" she asked.

"Ohhhh, yes. That was pretty, ehhh, impressive."

She pouted a bit and brushed her finger along the bottom of Nate's chin, knowing all too well the effect she was having upon him. "You watch all my fights, don't you?"

"Never miss a one."

"You know what my secret is?"

"You're real quick, I can tell you that."

She leaned in as Nate removed a bundle from his pocket. As her hand snaked out to take the bundle from him, she whispered, "I like to have a good, hard fuck before I go into a fight. Keeps me sharp."

Although Nate tried to respond to that, the only thing he managed to get out was a series of flustered mumbles. His head shook a little and he tried to form words, but wasn't having the slightest bit of luck.

Tia took the bundle, which was an envelope folded in two. She unfolded it, looked inside, and flipped through the money that was in there. Nodding, she said, "Looks like it was a good night."

"It suuure was. Well, still is. Are you going to be watching the rest of the fights? There's still a few more to go."

"Sure, I will."

"Maybe you'd, ehhh, like some company?"

"I'm a little tired right now. But check back with me tomorrow," she added with a wink. "I'll be getting ready for the next bout and all."

Nate's eyes widened anxiously and he nodded. Since he

couldn't come up with anything worth saying, he gave her an awkward salute and then headed back for the main tent.

Stuffing the envelope into her pocket, Tia walked back into the shadows where Clint was waiting.

"I think he likes you," Clint said sarcastically from where he was waiting.

"You think?"

"I also think you enjoy torturing that little rodent."

Now that she could make out where he was standing, Tia smirked at the shadowy outline of Clint's face. "I do need to get ready for my next fight tomorrow. What makes you think I've got anyone specific in mind just yet?"

Clint walked forward and put his hands on her hips. He savored the feel of her strong, solid curves and then took her bottom lip slowly into his mouth. Easing himself away from her, Clint said, "Just remember, I'm always willing to help a friend stay sharp."

Tia kept herself from showing just how excited that last kiss had gotten her. Then again, she wasn't able to do much else, and let Clint go without saying another word. She watched him move through the darkness like just another shadow, heading in the direction where Nate DeLouse had gone.

Shaking her head, Tia headed back into the main tent to keep from missing any more of the fights. Despite her interest in how the competition was faring, she couldn't stop thinking about the plans she had in store for Clint when she finally got her hands back on him.

THIRTY-TWO

With the fights in full swing, the few men standing around outside the main tent were either getting over a loss or too drunk to keep from falling into the pit. Nate DeLouse sidestepped those poor dregs with practiced ease as he tried to keep the scent of Tia's skin fresh in his mind.

He wasn't in a hurry to get back inside. Instead, he peeked into the largest entrance to the main tent just to make sure nobody was waiting for him. When all he saw were the backs of heads, he took a few steps from that door and dug into the inner pocket of his jacket.

Nate's hand emerged holding a small flask, which he opened and tipped to his lips. The liquid inside reached his tongue in a few drips before trickling down his throat. Already, the effects of the flask's contents could be felt in the back of Nate's mind.

"Saw you with that fighter," came a voice from a few feet away.

Nate looked over and saw a figure standing there with his hands in his pockets. The voice seemed vaguely familiar, but most everyone wanted Nate as their friend when it was fight night.

"Yeah. I talk to all the fighters."

"That one was pretty good," the voice continued. "Then again, that fighter was just plain pretty."

Nate smirked and nodded. "Oh, yeah."

"You get any luck with her?"

"Not, ehhhh, not yet."

"What about with Katrina Nolen? You seemed pretty damn lucky back in Carte Nueves."

Nate's eyes snapped open and he relaxed the hand that had been wrapped around his flask. The metal container slipped from his fingers as the man who'd been talking emerged from the shadows.

Clint took a quick step and snapped his hand out in a blur of motion. Just as quickly, he came to a stop, Nate's flask held in his outstretched hand.

Slowly, Clint lifted the flask to his nose and gave it a cautious sniff. "Absinthe? This is dangerous stuff, Nate. People tend to lose their minds if they drink too much of this."

The initial shock of seeing Clint was still written on Nate's face. When he tried to cover it up, the results were almost funny. "I know what I'm doing, Adams. I think the, ehhhh, real question here is . . . do you?"

"I know one thing. I know absinthe is a whole lot more expensive than the liquor served around here." With that, Clint tipped the flask and poured out the rest of the light green liquor that had been inside.

Nate watched and started to reach for the flask, but stopped when Clint slowly shook his head.

Once the last of the absinthe had trickled out, Clint smiled and handed back the flask to its owner. "There now," Clint said. "I might have just done you a service."

"Wh . . . what do you want?"

Instead of answering that question right away, Clint let Nate stew for a few moments.

"You've been real lucky so far, Louse."

Nate tried to collect himself, but failed miserably. His

words seeped out of him like water through a leaky bucket. "It's DeLouse. Dee-Loose."

"I think Louse fits you better. That all right with you?"

Nate didn't object.

"Like I said," Clint continued, "you've been pretty lucky. First, you got in good with Warren, and then you got your hands on a hell of a Grand Prize for Hackett's fights."

Nate shifted on his feet and started looking nervously around. "I wouldn't do anything to me if I were you. I'm pretty, ehhh, valuable around here."

"I know you are. That's why I wanted to have this little chat with you."

"If you want your gun back, you'll have to talk to Hackett."

Clint shook his head. "I'll get my gun back, but I know it's already out of your reach. I want to know what is going on with these fights. There's something that doesn't set right with me and I can't figure out what it is just yet."

"Something not right?"

Taking a few quick steps, Clint was able to position himself in front of Nate so that the smaller man was backed against a post. Clint looked down at him sternly, making sure that his face was the only thing Nate could see. "Don't bullshit me," Clint warned. "I heard that Warren and Katrina did what they did because of a debt owed to you. I saw you play cards in Carte Nueves and know for a fact you're not good enough to pile up a debt as big as all that."

"Cheat? Me? I, ehhh, just got lucky. That's it!"

"I never said you cheated, Nate. What's the matter? Guilty conscience?"

"Maybe I cheated a little, but never in our game," Nate quickly added. "I never cheated you, Adams, I swear."

"But you did cheat Warren?"

Nate nodded. "We had a few games a few days before sitting down with you. I got a few hands and then padded a few more. It wasn't anything serious, but it was enough to get me what I wanted."

"What you wanted? You mean a nice, healthy debt owed to you from Warren Nolen?"

Nate nodded again. It looked more like his head was trembling from the cold than anything else, but the intent was still easy enough to read. "Warren already owed a bundle to some other men on Mr. Hackett's payroll and I was just the one sent to push him over the edge.

"We just wanted to get Warren into these fights, but when he mentioned that his sister was going to pay you a visit, he said that he might be able to get something else instead."

Clint felt like he'd hit the soft spot in a dam and was watching more leak through than he'd ever thought possible. But rather than stop the flood of information coming from Nate's mouth, he kept it going with a simple, "Go on. I'm still listening."

Too late to turn back now, Nate slumped back against the post behind him as if that was the only thing holding him up. "These fights thrive on word of mouth, Mr. Adams. You must understand that. Putting up a prize like the pistol of The Gunsmith will make that word spread even farther than before. Already, we've got more bets flowing through here than ever before and fighters are really putting their best foot forward."

The faster Nate talked, the less he whined. It seemed that committing himself to what he was saying did him a bit of good. Either that, or he'd already convinced himself he was speaking the final words of his life. "Warren got out of Hackett's initial request, but he still showed up here in Mescall. That was a mistake, Adams. If you speak to Warren or care about what happens to him, you might want to tell him that."

"What was Hackett's initial request?"

Nate paused and looked at Clint as though he hadn't heard him correctly. "Warren was supposed to fight."

"Warren's a fighter?"

Shrugging, Nate replied, "He's as much of a fighter as any of the others that Mr. Hackett uses."

"Let me guess. Werner, Dilkins, and Offermann," Clint said, reciting the names he'd overheard when listening in on the conversation in Hackett's wagon. "They're the others working off debts to Hackett."

"Oh, so you do know about them."

"I do now."

THIRTY-THREE

The fights were just ending when Clint finally let Nate go. Clint was just about to head back into the main tent when he was nearly swept away by the stampede of men coming out of there. Rather than buck that tide, Clint hung back and waited for a familiar face to pass him by. When he saw who he was after, he reached in and plucked him out instead of trying to be heard over the noise of the crowd.

Rick Hartman struggled right up until he saw who was pulling him to the side. Then, he broke into a wide smile. "There you are, Clint! I was thinking you'd still be off with that lady fighter. Guess she got away from you, since she came back to place a few bets toward the end."

"Yeah, Rick. That's what happened."

"She sure knows her stuff," Hartman said happily. "We pulled in some good money between the two of us. I made a bundle on the fight right after hers, and nearly lost twice as much on the next one, but she kept me from making the bet I wanted to make. I thought I had those names figured out." Glancing around suspiciously, Hartman added, "You know. Those names we heard?"

Clint was still more concerned about finding a spot where they might not be overheard. Pulling away from the flow of people headed for the saloons, he picked out a spot that would fit the bill for a minute or two. "I remember the names."

"Well, I thought they were the winners, then it seemed they were losers. After Offermann nearly killed a man in the fourth fight, I don't know what the hell those names were."

Finally, Clint came to a stop somewhere where they weren't about to be knocked over by a flood of rowdy drunks. "I know what those names are."

"Really? How'd you find that out?"

"I had a little chat with the Louse," Clint explained.

"And you think you can believe a word that asshole has to say?"

"Normally, no. This time, let's just say he wasn't in a spot where lying was in his best interest."

Hartman smiled and nodded. "I like the sound of that. What'd the Louse say about those names?"

"They're men roped into fighting to work off debts owed to Hackett or one of his men. I had a good, long talk with Nate and he said that Hackett's even got some professional sharps on his payroll to get some prime candidates in a deep enough hole to land them in the pit."

"Seems like an odd way to recruit fighters."

"That's what I thought. Especially since everyone seems so fired up to be here. Tia acted like it was an honor to jump in that pit and start swinging punches."

Hartman shrugged and said, "Of course, being here to watch these things is a hell of a big deal. Fighting in them may be something else."

"You think you could get in and have a chat with one of the fighters?" Clint asked. "Maybe one or two that weren't on the list?"

"You've got yourself an inside track on one of those fighters yourself," Hartman said with a nudge.

"Yeah, and I'll talk to her. I'll also see about having a

word with some of the names that are on that list. While
I'm at it, I may have another word or two with Hackett. He
seems to be open for a discussion."

"Oh, sure, just as long as it's on his terms and he's surrounded by his guns."

"Which is exactly why I don't want you along for that
one. If things get messy, there's no need for you to get
hurt."

"Appreciate it, Clint, but I didn't just come all this way
for the betting."

There was no mistaking the resolve in Hartman's tone.
Clint knew well enough how difficult it was to turn the
Texan in another direction once he had his heart set on
something. When personal loyalties came into the mix, he
got even more bullheaded.

"You want to help out?" Clint asked. "Then see what you
can find out about why these fighters are here. Along the way,
you're bound to trip across plenty of useful information."

Hartman laughed under his breath. "All this trouble just
to get your gun back, huh? Is this how it always is for you?"

"Now you see why I'm gone for so long at a stretch."

"I knew you tended to attract trouble, but damn, I don't
even see how you have enough time to catch any sleep."

"Then do me a favor and try to keep your head down. You
can handle yourself, so don't put yourself in anyone's line
of fire. Usually, when you start poking into the affairs of
men like Hackett, they tend to get a little resentful about it."

"You could always leave them alone, you know. Maybe
then you'd spend less time dodging bullets."

Clint smirked and asked, "Now how much fun is that?"

Hartman shook his head and let out a frustrated sigh.
"I'll see what I can see. Actually, I think I recognize a few
of these fighters from boxing matches or other events that
came through West Texas at one time or another."

"Great. Buy them a drink and I'm sure you won't have
any trouble getting them to talk."

"Hey, I own a saloon, remember? Let me handle the talkative drunks and I'll let you handle the shotgun-toting gorillas. Deal?"

Clint shook the hand Hartman offered and nodded. "It's a deal. We'll try to meet up at the stables where our horses are being kept every three hours."

Both men checked their watches and agreed on the time for the next meeting. From there, they split up and started walking toward different sections of camp.

Before getting too far away, Hartman stopped and hollered back at Clint, "Just remember, if all else fails you made a pretty damn fine piece of hardware to fill that holster. Fetching the original ain't exactly worth risking your life."

"I know, Hartman. I just don't think my life is the only one at stake anymore."

Hartman shook his head and waved at Clint dismissively. "I knew you'd say something like that."

THIRTY-FOUR

"Mr. Adams!" boomed a voice that was familiar to anyone at the fights earlier that night. "Come on in!"

Dale Hackett was in good spirits. One of the smaller tents in Mescall had been cleared out so the big man could sit down to a good meal. The rest of the camp was alive and kicking up plenty of dust as gamblers and fighters alike all filled the saloons so they could fill their bellies on anything served to them in a mug.

Clint had taken it upon himself to find Hackett while he was still reveling in the night's success. It had only taken him a few minutes to do just that.

"I was just gonna send for you," Hackett bellowed. "How'd you find me?"

Clint stepped into the tent, which was only big enough to hold four small tables. Hackett sat at the table in the middle, surrounded by half a dozen of his shotgun-wielding guards.

"Finding you wasn't too hard," Clint said. "All I needed to do was look for the firepower."

Hackett shrugged and pulled a roll in half. "When I first started running this affair, I tried holding everyone's guns while they were here. That didn't work out too well, so I just make it a real good idea for folks to keep themselves in check."

"Yeah, I saw that firsthand with those fellas who tried to look me up."

"It works. Why don't you have a seat and join me for supper? You have anything to eat yet?"

Before Clint could answer, another place was set for him and a young man in dirty clothes rushed out to pile up some food onto a plate. It was a mess of potatoes, peas, and chopped steak, but it smelled better than anything else in the camp.

Well, Clint thought as he remembered his recent time with Tia, almost anything else.

"Thanks," Clint said as he took his seat. "I am a bit hungry."

"Great! I've been meaning to catch up with you since you've been here. What do you think of Mescall?"

"It's not too bad. Sure seems like you're pulling in a pile of cash."

"I do all right, but so does everyone else. You should consider being a partner. I'm sure it would be to your advantage."

"Sorry," Clint replied. "But I don't partner up with someone who steals from me."

Hackett nodded and sopped up some gravy with his roll. "Ah, you're talking about the pistol."

"For starters."

After stuffing the roll into his mouth, Hackett shrugged. "Sorry, Adams, but that pistol came into my possession and it's too late to do anything about it now. Of course, there is one way for you to get it back."

Smirking, Clint took a bite of his meal and washed it down with some water that had been placed onto the table. "Let me guess. You want me to fight for it?"

Hackett nodded. "It'd be one hell of a fight. Just think of

it, Adams. The percentages from the betting alone would make us rich."

"How do you figure?"

"Easy! I get a piece of all the action here, plus there'd be side bets and Lord only knows how many others would—"

"No," Clint interrupted. "How do you figure on me entering a contest to win back what's rightfully mine?"

"That's easy," Hackett said in a tone that had suddenly become more than a little dark. "It's the only way there is. I sure as hell aren't just going to hand it over. As far as I know, that may not even be your gun."

"Then why bother with it?"

"How much do you think any trophy's worth? It's about status, Adams. In the end, that's every fighter's currency."

"What about survival?" Clint asked after stabbing a piece of beef with his fork. "That's always a pretty powerful bargaining chip."

Hackett glanced up and studied Clint's face. It was a cold, calculating look that made Clint understand how a chicken felt when it was about to go on the chopping block.

"You got something else you want to say?" Hackett asked.

The conversation was being played like a hand of poker. Each player had made a few moves and studied each other as best they could. Clint had tried to get Hackett to spill some more information, but the bait hadn't been taken. That, alone, told Clint something else about the man he was dealing with.

"I've heard that not all of the fighters in your matches are exactly professionals," Clint said.

Hackett shrugged. "That's no secret. Anyone's allowed to toss their hat into the ring."

"Must be tough to get so many fighters to fill such a busy schedule. From what I've seen, it looks like there were fights going on for days before the main event started."

"There are fights going on every hour of every day in Mescall. When the fights stop, Mescall disappears."

"And that brings me to something else that doesn't quite sit well with me. Why is it that there are so many other fights that are held and yours has to travel around and hide like a gypsy caravan?" Clint watched Hackett's reaction as he took another bite of potatoes. "Actually," Clint continued, "even gypsies don't have to hide as much as you do. What's the problem, Hackett? What are you trying to keep so secret?"

"I don't know if I like where this is headed, Adams."

"Neither do I. Especially since I've heard that you've been forcing men to fight to work off debts that they got tricked into owing."

"I think it's time for you to leave."

Clint could feel Hackett's growing tension like a storm coming up on the horizon. Despite the fact that the shotgunners nearby were responding to Hackett as well, Clint kept pushing.

"This is a big business for you," Clint said. "You've said yourself how much money you make off your percentage of the betting profits. You must also get a piece of the food, beds, and women that are sold around here as well."

"Of course I do. What's your point?"

"It just tells me how important it must be for you to keep these fights going. You can't exactly rake in all that cash if the main reason for Mescall's existence dries up and blows away. Is that why you stock your fights with men you suckered into spilling their blood for a cheering crowd?"

Hackett was still gripping his knife in his hand, but looked as though the last thing he wanted to stab was the food on his plate. His eyes burned in their sockets and his teeth started grinding together. "You want your gun, Adams? You talk to the one who wins it."

Clint shook his head and smiled at the way Hackett was starting to squirm. "Too late for that. I've already got myself some new iron."

"Then take it and get the hell out of here."

"What's the matter? You don't want to chat anymore?"

"I don't like men who don't know their place." Lifting a hand, Hackett snapped his fingers once and brought three of his shotgunners forward. "Mescall isn't a town with rules or law. It's a kingdom and what I say goes. You don't step into any kingdom and talk to the king the way you're talking to me."

THIRTY-FIVE

The three men holding shotguns pointed at Clint were giving him a look that said they had every intention of pulling their triggers. They all smiled at him and waited to hear the order from Hackett. As the eagerness built in their eyes, it wasn't even a sure bet that they would wait for that order.

"You're no king, Hackett. You're a thief and a swindler. Nothing more."

Sensing his men behind him, Hackett raised his hand to keep them in check. His eyes narrowed as they focused on Clint with a mix of disbelief and admiration. "What happened, Adams?" he asked without the anger that had been in his voice moments ago. "Did a friend of yours wind up in the pit?"

Clint shook his head. "Not exactly, but I would like to know about Warren Nolen. You recognize that name?"

Hackett thought it over and then smirked. "Oh, yeah. He's the boy that handed over that fancy gun of yours to Nate. He's got some good ideas, that kid. Can't play cards for shit, but he's got some good ideas."

"Was he supposed to be in that pit as well?"

"Yeah. He was."

"And do you think he would have stood a chance against the fighters you've got in there?"

"Nope, but that's what makes for such a good show."

And there it was.

That statement, alone, told Clint everything he needed to know. It tipped Hackett's hand to show the true man he was.

"You toss those men you tricked into that pit just so they can bleed," Clint said. "They might win and they might lose, but you put them in there so they can be backed into a corner and fight for their lives, all so you can keep up the excitement in your fights. That's all it is?"

Hackett nodded. "It's a show, Adams. The fighters have their reasons for being here, but there's not enough of them to go around. I found that out for myself when I nearly went out of business a few years ago.

"You see, back then I used to run my fights as a bareknuckle tournament and nothing else. It did pretty well, but there was competition from other fights as well as that certain factor that no other sport has to deal with.

"Fighters aren't racehorses," Hackett said as though he was teaching a class on the subject. "They're savages who'll kill themselves to win a goddamn belt or some cheap piece of trash with their name on it. They fight with their hearts and souls and tear each other to pieces in the process.

"You know why they tossed Christians to the lions, Adams? Because Christians aren't going to hurt the lions the way the lions would hurt themselves in that same arena. At least, that's how I figure because I ran into the same problem. My fighters started dying on me and even though that made for some exciting matches, it wasn't good for the long run."

The shotgunners were closing in around Clint from all sides by now. What disturbed Clint even more than that, however, was the fact that Hackett no longer seemed concerned about anything at all. He was once again King of Mescall and looked down on Clint as he would any other peasant.

"I don't force anyone to gamble," Hackett continued smugly. "But I am a businessman and that means taking advantage wherever I can. Those idiots who owe me their land and life savings would have lost those things somewhere else eventually. At least I give them a chance to get out of debt without taking their property. I don't want any of those ranches or farms or houses that are owed to me, but I do want men to fight in Mescall."

"Christians to feed to your lions," Clint said.

Hackett nodded and pointed a finger across the table. "Exactly. And I run my little coliseum here in a way that makes more money every time I set up my tents. My lions stay healthy and only bite at each other when it's absolutely necessary. I've even picked up a few new lions along the way with my little system. Some of those bad gamblers have actually turned into good fighters."

Hackett sat up proudly and stated, "I truly do give men second chances. They either shine or they burn out. Either way, at least they're not just deadweight any more. So what do you say, Adams? You want to throw in and make some money with me or step into the pit and give these folks the show of their lives to win your precious gun back?"

"Are those the only choices?"

"No," Hackett said as the guards all brought their shotguns up. "But I don't think you'll like your third choice."

THIRTY-SIX

Clint pushed away from the table and got to his feet. He could feel the weight of the pistol at his side, but didn't let his hand get too close to it just yet. He'd already sized up the guards in that tent and knew that if he so much as twitched in the wrong direction, they would all pull their triggers and cut him down in a heartbeat.

That was the bad thing about shotguns. At close range, they were a force to be reckoned with in anyone's hands.

Although noises and voices drifted in from outside the tent, the silence inside it was thick enough to be cut with a knife. Every so often, Clint swore he could hear the creak of fingers slowly tensing around triggers.

Finally, Clint lifted his hands to chest level. He kept them open and steady to signal his good intentions to the rest of the guards. "I didn't come in here to start trouble," he said.

"And I don't want trouble with you, Adams," Hackett countered. "Getting your gun was a twist of fate. I'm sure you understand that I can't put it up as a prize and then take it away again. That would just make me look bad."

Clint nodded and turned toward the opening that led out

of the tent. "So are your guards going to move or do they want trouble, too?"

At the sound of another snap of Hackett's fingers, the two guards in front of Clint grudgingly stepped aside.

"Think about my offer, Adams," Hackett said to Clint's back. "We could still be partners. At the very least, we could both make a hell of a lot of money if you agreed to fight to get your gun back. I could assure you that you'd have a better-than-average chance of winning."

Although Clint paused for a moment, he stepped out of the tent and kept walking. Every guard in there watched and waited for Clint to come back. Their hands were itching on their shotguns, and they were visibly disappointed when it was obvious that Clint had left them for good.

"Let him go," Hackett said to the guards. "He won't be going far."

Without making a sound, Hackett locked eyes with the guard closest to the door and nodded toward the opening. That guard leaned outside and took a few steps out.

After a few seconds, the guard came back and said, "He's gone."

"Take a few others and follow him," Hackett commanded. "Don't let Adams see you, but don't you let him out of your sight, either. Make sure he doesn't do anything that he's not supposed to. And, for God's sake, keep him away from the fighters. If Adams says more than a how-do-you-do to one of those sides of beef, you steer him in another direction. Understand me?"

"I understand," the man replied with an anxious sneer.

The guard who'd been at the back of the room stepped forward so that he had both Hackett and the front of the tent in his sights. "He knows an awful lot about the way things are run around here."

"That's because he's a smart man, Cal."

"What should we do about it?"

Hackett sighed and picked at his food some more. Finally, he took another bite and then pushed his plate away. "We give him a chance to think things over and make a move. He found out a bit more than I was hoping, but he wasn't stupid enough to do much about it. I've dealt with his kind before. Unless there's enough in it for him, he won't be stepping too far out of line."

Cal wasn't the biggest of Hackett's guards, but he had more going on behind his eyes. While the others waited for orders and a chance to use their shotguns, Cal was taking in every detail of his surroundings without doing anything to make himself stand out in the crowd. "What about that gun of his?"

Hackett let out a snorting laugh. "It was enough to get him here, but it's not enough for him to risk getting killed."

"Why'd you bother with that?"

"What did you say?" Hackett asked as he leveled a mean stare in the other man's direction.

Cal took a moment to think over his choice of words, but he didn't falter for very long. "That gun seems to be more trouble than it was worth. Why don't we just give it back and make that asshole Warren pay us what he owes? At least that way we wouldn't have to worry about Adams poking his nose around where it doesn't belong."

Hackett smiled and approached Cal. Shifting to a condescending tone, he asked, "Did you happen to get a look at the amount of money we've been pulling in?"

"Of course. It's been pretty good."

"Pretty good? It's been downright amazing! The men around here may or may not believe that I've got The Gunsmith's pistol, but they sure as hell have been talking about it. Do you think it's a coincidence that there's not a single cot to be rented in Mescall? Do you think it's a coincidence that this place is busting at the seams now that I've announced the prize? Folks have been riding in from damn near every town in range and I'd bet that there will only be more coming every day.

"This is shaping up to be one of the best events I've ever had and it's all got to do with word of mouth. People aren't here to win Clint Adams's gun. They're here because word has spread that Adams, himself, is here and they all want to get a look at The Gunsmith with their own eyes on the chance that they might see him fight to get back his property."

Cal let out a weary breath and said, "That's a dangerous gamble. The Gunsmith didn't get his reputation by being as stupid as you think he is."

"I don't think he's stupid at all. He's here and that's all that matters. This is enough free advertising to make my next six events into gold mines!"

"And what if Adams does step out of line?" Cal asked.

"Then we give these people a show they couldn't imagine." Holding up his hands to frame an imaginary poster, Hackett declared, "The death of The Gunsmith. Now how's that for a main event?"

THIRTY-SEVEN

Clint met up with Rick Hartman at the designated time and place. All of Mescall was crawling with every kind of humanity in all states of sobriety. The ground was damp with a stinking mixture of spilled beer, liquor, blood, and worse. The air was a chaotic jumble of raised voices ranging from screams to laughter to singing.

"Jesus Christ," Hartman said when he saw Clint approach. "Now I see why I don't go to these things every time they come around. This place is a madhouse."

"Well, don't let your guard down on my account. I'm being followed." When he saw Hartman start to glance around, Clint stopped him. "Don't look. They're behind me and they have been ever since I left from my talk with Hackett. Just let them think they're doing their job."

"You talked to Hackett?"

"Yeah. Did you get a chance to meet up with any of those fighters, yet?"

Hartman chuckled and replied, "The tricky part is trying to go somewhere and not run into one of the fighters. Even the losers are strutting around here like roosters."

"All of them?"

"Not every last one, but a good amount of them. Why?"

Clint relayed his conversation with Hackett as quickly as he could.

"He stocks the fights, huh?" Hartman asked. "I guess that explains the list of names we heard. He was just making sure those men showed up to fulfill their part of the deal."

"Did you see any of those men when you were out and about?"

Hartman thought that over and then shook his head. "Now that you mention it, those fellows weren't to be seen. Except for Offermann, that is. He seems to be taking to this life just fine since he did beat his opponent to a pulp earlier tonight. I also saw that redhead of yours. She's buying enough rounds to keep this whole camp three sheets to the wind."

"I don't think anyone's twisting her arm to fight," Clint mused. Shaking his head to put himself back on track, he said, "I need you to find out where those other fighters are staying."

"The ones on Hackett's list?"

"That's right. There's bound to be plenty more of them that we didn't hear mentioned before because there are sure plenty more fights to go before Mescall is packed up and moved to the next open field."

Hartman nodded. "Shouldn't be too hard. I actually had to pull myself away from a group of fighters so I could meet up with you here. They're basically a good bunch of fellas."

"Sure they are. Those are the ones who want to be here. These fights might not be aboveboard, but I've got no problem with the legitimate fighters. It's the other ones that concern me. Those others might be stupid and unlucky, but they don't deserve to get themselves killed just to appease a bunch of screaming drunks."

"Sounds like you already heard about the discovery I made," Hartman said.

"What discovery?"

"The final round of the fights," Hartman explained. When he saw the confused expression remaining on Clint's face, he said, "You know. The round with the most expensive seats."

"Just spit it out, Rick."

Realizing that he still had something that Clint hadn't found out about, Hartman leaned in and quickly started talking again. "I thought for certain Hackett would have told you about this or that you found out about it on your own.

"Anyway, I heard from one of the fighters that all of these pit fights are just elimination rounds to see who goes on to the real event. It's a fight to the death, Clint. Most folks around here don't know about it, but the ones that do keep it to themselves. Rich ranchers and business types come to Mescall on the night when Hackett is supposed to be folding his tents. That's the night the real blood is spilled."

Clint nodded grimly. "And I'll wager that's the night when Hackett truly settles his debts with more than a few of those unlucky gamblers."

"I don't know about that for certain," Hartman said. "But the fighters I talked to said that the losers of the fights on that last night either wind up dead or close to it. They don't speak about it too much because that's the sort of thing that could get them in trouble with the law."

"Maybe they should be in trouble with the law if they're killers. Using a gun or their bare hands doesn't make much difference after it's all said and done."

Hartman shook his head. "Not all the fighters take part in those last rounds. Just the real bloodthirsty ones and a few of Hackett's own guards."

"Yeah? Well, they sure do know a lot about it."

"They talk amongst themselves, Clint. Just like we're doing here and now."

"You sound like you're defending them, Rick."

"The fellas I talked to aren't killers," Hartman replied earnestly.

Clint studied his friend's face and didn't see a trace of deception. He didn't have any reason to doubt Hartman's word, but the blood was still flowing hot through his veins after his talk with Hackett.

Letting out a deep breath, Clint relaxed a bit and patted Hartman's shoulder. "If you say the men you talked to are all right, then I believe you," Clint said. "But I intend on finding out for myself which ones are killers and which just like to crack skulls for a living. We're going to be at that last round of fights."

"I had a notion you'd be saying that."

"And since we're going, I'd say that means there are a few people who won't have to show up," Clint added with a mischievous grin. "Do your best to find out where those fighters are who were duped into being here. Round them up and either bring them here or bring me to them when we meet up again."

Hartman was already smiling. "Actually, that was my next bit of news I wanted to share. I already know where those others are being kept."

"You were busy," Clint said with admiration.

Hartman shrugged. "Hey, I tend bar for a living. I know how to get folks to tell me things that they would normally take to their grave. Of course, with all the liquor flowing around here, it wasn't too hard."

"What are we waiting for?" Clint asked. "Let's pay them a visit."

THIRTY-EIGHT

The section of Mescall where Rick Hartman took Clint was on one of the unlabeled sections of the map they'd bought. On first glance, it was an uninteresting row of covered wagons sitting among a few leaning tents. There were people standing around in the shadows, but they kept to themselves and discouraged anyone approaching them with narrow, intense glares.

The rest of the camp was getting rowdier by the minute and the sounds drifting through the air seemed like enough to wake the dead. As they moved between the wagons and approached the cluster of dark tents, Clint and Hartman knew they were being followed.

They'd been followed all the way from the stables where they'd met up. Clint had been sure to point out the men on their tail with a few subtle nods. Hartman didn't have much trouble spotting them, since they were some of the only sober faces in the vicinity. To a bartender, that was a better marker than if those guards had been waving torches in both hands.

They were well into the outskirts of Mescall when Clint gave Hartman a nod and made a sharp turn. As they'd arranged shortly after leaving the stable, Hartman and

Clint split off from each other without so much as a word passing between them.

The guards following them started to split up, but paused to have a quick word amongst themselves. It didn't take long for them to decide on a course of action. Two of them headed in Clint's direction, while the third took off after Hartman.

They quickly ran into one problem, however.

Both Clint and Hartman had disappeared.

All three men chased shadows that they thought were the men they were after, but that wound up being nothing more than ghosts. The night was dark enough, and got even darker now that the torches and lanterns of the main camp were a good distance away.

The suspicious eyes that had been there before were still there now, watching the guards without making a sound or lifting a finger to help them.

"Hey," the guard who'd been attempting to follow Hartman said. "You there. Sitting by that tent. Did you see a man walk by here just now?"

When he got no reply, the guard stepped forward and snarled at the figure in the shadows.

"I'm talking to you, asshole. You want to answer or would you like me to jam this shotgun up your ass?"

Sitting in the darkness was a man with fresh cuts on his face that glistened wetly in the trickle of moonlight that reached him. When he smiled, his newly chipped teeth glinted as well. "Try looking behind you."

Hearing that, the guard shot a look over his shoulder and found himself staring directly into Clint's face. His first impulse was to turn around so he could take aim with his shotgun. Halfway through that motion, his arms were stopped by a solid grip.

Clint reached out and grabbed hold of the guard's elbow as he lunged forward. With his other hand, he sought out and found the shotgun, which he then pulled free of the guard's hands.

Instead of realizing he was already beat, the guard balled up a fist and sent it into Clint's gut. He felt his knuckles bury themselves into Clint's midsection and heard the satisfying wheeze as Clint's breath was pushed from his lungs. The next thing the guard felt was the barrel of his own shotgun press up against his chin.

"You took your shot," Clint snarled as he thumbed back the shotgun's hammers. "You want me to take mine?"

"N . . . no, sir."

"Good thinking. Now call the other ones over here."

Clint could feel the guard start to build up his confidence, but all it took was a little more pressure behind the shotgun to nip that in the bud.

"Hey!" the guard shouted. "Over here! I found them."

The two guards who'd been trying to find Clint came bounding into sight wearing exasperated looks on their faces. They hadn't even spotted the figure in the shadows coming right up behind them.

"Where are they?" one of the guards asked when he caught sight of their partner. "Who's that with you?"

Suddenly, the figure in the shadows reached out and grabbed hold of one of the guards to pull him off to one side. The guard was dragged down and relieved of his shotgun before he knew what was happening and just when he got a look at Hartman's face, he was feeling Hartman's boot press down against his throat.

Hartman was all smiles as he subdued the guard. Pointing the shotgun at the man in front of Clint, he said, "I got this one. The third scampered off. You'd best chase him down before he gets reinforcements."

But Clint hadn't moved. Instead, his eyes were tracking over all the shapes that had emerged from the shadows to surround them. "Um, it looks like the reinforcements are already here."

THIRTY-NINE

The figures were everywhere.

Like shadows that had split off from every wall and every surface, they surrounded Clint and Hartman to loom over them menacingly. It wasn't long before those shadows moved in and got close enough for their faces to be seen.

"Hand them over," one of the shadows said. "Now."

Clint stood up while keeping the shotgun in his hand aimed at the guard. "I won't let you do this, Warren. You've already gotten into enough trouble."

Warren Nolen moved forward another few steps, glaring at the guards with the eyes of a starving animal. All the other men flanking Warren had that same look on their faces. It was a look that had been earned in the pit.

"These bastards ruined my life," Warren said. "They ruined all our lives."

The two guards were starting to squirm and Clint was more than happy to let them. The guards squirmed even more once another couple of fighters stormed into the group, dragging the third guard between them.

"Look what we found," one of the fighters said.

The other fighter carrying the third guard looked straight

at Clint and said, "We went after him, just like you said. What should we do with him, Mr. Adams?"

"You know who I am?" Clint asked.

There were nods all around.

"You know where you can get some rope?"

More nods, only this time they were twice as enthusiastic.

"Get some rope and tie them up," Clint said. "Gag their mouths and keep them quiet."

"That's not good enough," Warren said. "They need to bleed for what they done."

Hartman looked over to the young gambler and asked, "What are you even doing here, Warren? I thought you squared your debt when you brought in Clint's gun."

"So did I," Warren replied with more than a little shame in his voice. "But it wasn't enough."

"It's never enough!" one of the other fighters shouted. "I lost half my land and all my mules to that bloodsucker and I still got to fight for him if my family is to keep the rest of the farm."

"I lost all my land," piped up another. "And Hackett threatened to pay a visit to my daughters if I didn't take part in this madness."

But Clint's eyes were still on Warren. He saw something in that one's eyes that burned brighter than any of the others. It was a rage that nearly put all the others to shame.

"What happened, Warren?" Clint asked.

Everyone fell silent so Warren could be heard. The young man looked up and said, "Hackett's got my sister. He took Katrina and said he'd only give her back once I fight in the last round that's to take place in a few days."

Clint looked at the faces of the men gathering around him. "How many of you are to take part in the last round of fights?"

Every one of the men raised their hands.

"Then most of you probably won't walk out of there,"

Clint told them. "And the ones that do will have more blood on your hands than you know what to do with. Hackett's last round of fights is to the death. That's why he's forced you all into the situations you're in right now."

Clint's words stirred up plenty of backlash. Although there was a good amount of venom in the voices growling in the darkness, there wasn't much disbelief. All of the fighters had been through enough to know that Hackett wasn't beyond going one step further.

"What the hell do we do?" one of the fighters asked. "If I don't fight, my home goes up in flames. My wife'll probably burn, too!"

"He's got the deed to my land."

"And the papers to give him ownership of my store."

The voices came from all directions. Each of them told Clint a story that was harder to hear than the last. All of them were stories of loss, and just as many involved losing friends or loved ones as involved losing property or land. It wasn't long at all before Clint had heard enough.

"Hackett's main edge is that he kept this from you men," Clint said. "I doubt he's truly got enough hired guns to watch over every last one of those things or people."

"Maybe we don't want to take that chance."

Clint didn't even hear who'd said that. He simply replied to the group as a whole. "No matter what, it all revolves around Hackett and he's here."

"Yeah," Warren said. "And so's my sister."

"How many others here have loved ones here in Mescall or in a town nearby that you're worried about?"

Only a few of the men raised their hands.

"Then the rest of you leave."

Everyone looked at Clint as if he'd sprouted antlers.

"What?" one of the fighters asked.

"Leave," Clint repeated. "When are the next fights where you men will be involved?"

"Tomorrow night," Warren said. "The rest of the fights between now and then are between the real fighters."

Clint nodded and spoke with a commanding tone. "Then the rest of you leave. Go take your land back and look in on your loved ones. Collect the law along the way and bring them with you. The best Hackett's got is probably a few scouts here and there to let him know what's going on.

"We're out in the middle of nowhere right now so there's no way for him to get any news from the outside world. Besides, he's so wrapped up in these fights right now that he doesn't care about much else. I'm telling you, Hackett expects you men to either wind up dead or too scared to say anything once this is over. I've seen that in his eyes."

"How can you be so certain?" one of the men asked. "What if you're wrong?"

"Hackett's a bag of wind hiding behind a lot of shotguns. I've seen that in his eyes, too."

"And so what if he is wrong?" Hartman chimed in. "From the sound of it, I'd say you don't have much else to lose. You men are scared and you all have good reason to be. But the worst has already happened and right now, everything you're trying to protect is sitting alone and unprotected. Get back to where you're needed and take care of your business."

Clint nodded and placed his hand upon the gun holstered at his side. It was a simple thing, but it drew plenty of eyes toward that firearm. "Hackett's men were posted nearby to keep an eye on you. They might have come to do something if you'd tried to leave or they might have gone out to follow up on some of those threats. But we're here to tell you that you are all here just to line Hackett's pockets and the only way for you to get your lives back is if you ride out and take them back.

"You men that have no ties here go now and take care of your business. The others who have more immediate concerns," Clint added while laying a hand on Warren's shoulder, "stay strong and follow my lead when the time comes."

"No," one of the fighters said. "I want to stay."

"Me, too."

"And me."

"To hell with Hackett!"

That sentiment worked its way through the men until Clint had to quiet them down. "So, is it unanimous?"

It was.

Clint nodded and looked at all the eager fighters around him. "Then this might just be easier than I thought."

FORTY

The skies over Mescall were just starting to show the first traces of dawn. Having spent enough time in the camp, Clint felt like the last thing he needed was sleep. Despite the crowds of drunks and loud-talking fighters, the energy in the air was undeniable. It could even be felt when the only fights happening were the ones in the saloons.

Clint didn't have any trouble finding Tia. She was in the saloon where the rest of the fighters drank, and was laughing with the burly men as if she didn't know she might be trading punches with them soon. Those fighters were the professionals. That much could be seen in the proud way they wore their scars and displayed the blood on their teeth.

The moment she saw him, Tia rushed out to wrap her arms around Clint. Although it wasn't too bad, the smell of whiskey on her breath was enough to catch his attention.

"There you are, Clint! I've been waiting to see you all night. The boys and I wanted to ask you about the rumors we heard about you."

"Sure thing. I can buy a round of drinks tomorrow." Clint led her away from the saloon and toward the rows of tents reserved for sleeping. "Is there somewhere we can talk?"

"Do you mean really talk? Or talk until we find something better to do?"

"Really talk." The seriousness in Clint's voice was enough to cut through Tia's playful mood.

She sobered up instantly and nodded. "All right. I've got a place that we can have all to ourselves."

Taking him by the hand, she led Clint past the tents and to the edge of camp. There, sitting close to a corral fashioned from a few stakes and rope tied between them, was a covered wagon that looked like it might have been used in the first Gold Rush.

Tia hopped into the back of the wagon and Clint did the same. Inside, the wagon had Tia's belongings wrapped up in bundles lining either side. Laid out in the middle was a thick collection of blankets that was surprisingly comfortable when Clint sat down with her on them.

"What's the big secret?" she asked.

"I just wanted to tell you that I know about the final rounds of the fights being held here." Clint studied her face and saw a little glint of acknowledgment.

"They're being held soon," she said. "It's on the schedule."

"No," Clint said. "I mean the round with the smaller audience and bigger admission price."

Nodding, she said, "We're not supposed to let on about that. It gets kind of rough and some of it isn't exactly legal."

"Men have died in those fights."

"Only the ones that can't handle themselves. Look, don't worry about me. I've survived plenty of them and I make sure not to hurt anyone too badly. About the only difference is that we use weapons in those fights. Not guns, but knives and such."

"And what about the deaths? How do you explain those?"

Tia shrugged. "I don't need to explain those. The fighters that get involved in those matches go in knowing what to expect. There have been plenty of boxers killed in regular fights, too, you know. Nobody's forcing us to go in there, Clint. It's what we do."

Years of reading people across a poker table as well as watching the eyes of killers before they went for their guns had taught Clint to recognize bullshit when he heard it. Tia wasn't even close to lying to him. He'd suspected as much, but now he knew for sure.

"Nobody may be forcing you or most of the other professionals," Clint said. "But there's plenty of men in there who are being forced."

"What are you talking about?"

Clint told her exactly what he was talking about. In fact, he laid down everything for her, starting from his first meeting with Hackett and ending with his recent conversation with the other group of fighters. Tia didn't seem too surprised to hear a lot of what Clint had to say. That changed, however, when he got to the part about how Hackett recruited some of his fighters.

"Are you serious?" she asked.

Clint nodded. "Afraid so. Did you know about any of that?"

"About Hackett roping poor fools into fighting and dying for money? Hell, no, I didn't know. What kind of person do you take me for?"

"I already had a pretty good idea what kind of person you were. Glad to see I was right."

Tia smiled and rubbed Clint's cheek affectionately. Her expression turned grim, however, when she said, "We need to do something about this. A fighter's life's not easy, and it shouldn't be forced on anyone. At least, not when it comes to the fights in that last round."

"My thoughts exactly. Do you think any of the others you know are aware of what's going on?"

"Honestly, there's got to be a few who know. But I can think of around half a dozen that would tear Hackett apart if they knew what was going on. They'll be crushed to know they were beating on someone just trying to protect their families."

Tia pounded a fist against the wagon's floor beneath her. "I got used and so did most of my friends. Hackett can't get away with this. As a matter of fact," she said while crawling toward the wagon's exit, "I think I'll have a nice little chat with Hackett right now."

Clint reached out and took hold of Tia's arm. It required a good amount of his strength, but he was able to pull her back into the wagon. She landed in a heap in his lap. "Before you go charging off, you should hear what I've got in mind."

"Hackett deserves some payback for what he's done to everyone here," she said in a rush. "And his men need to pay for roping in those poor souls. And I want to know which of the real fighters knew about this so I can pay them back, too."

"Trust me, I agree with you wholeheartedly. But I've got a way to cover all of those scores." Now that he had her attention, Clint spelled out the same basic plan he'd spelled out to Warren Nolen and the men in that remote section of Mescall.

Tia listened grudgingly at first, but soon settled in and stopped trying to get out of the wagon. Before too long, she was soaking up every word Clint said, and even started leaning in to make sure she didn't miss a bit of it. When he was done, Clint watched her face to get a feel for how she might react.

He didn't have to wait very long.

"Now that," she said with a smile that grew like wildfire with every word she said, "is what I call a plan! Do you think those others will agree to it?"

"They volunteered."

Nodding, Tia knocked her fist against the floor to work out the anxiousness that was building inside her.

Clint couldn't help but smile, himself, just by being so close to her. "I figure this way, you can see for yourself what Hackett's done."

"I always knew there was something about him, but men who arrange fights like these are never really the best of sorts. When does all this start?"

"Tomorrow night."

"I like it," Tia said as she slipped her arms around Clint's neck and brushed her lips against it. "I like it a lot."

FORTY-ONE

Clint could feel the heat from Tia's body soaking through their clothes to warm him all the way down to the bone. She pressed against him and started brushing her tongue along the side of his neck.

"You sure this is the right time for this?" Clint forced himself to ask.

Tia kept up what she was doing as she replied, "It's about dawn right now and you said you wouldn't be doing anything until afternoon, right?"

"That's right."

"Then we've got time and your plan means I've got a fight on the way."

Clint wasn't able to stop himself all the way. His hands were roaming over her body and his lips were close to her ear as he whispered, "Probably."

"And I already told you how I prepare for a fight."

"You know something? Maybe I should give that a shot, myself."

Scooping her up into his arms, Clint laid Tia down on the blankets and positioned himself on top of her. They were both shrugging out of their clothes and tossing them into piles all around the wagon. There was barely enough room for them to maneuver in there, but that only made it better as they bumped against each other while undressing.

After a bit of squirming, they were both naked and picking right up where they'd left off. Clint had gotten a good feel for her body the first time they'd been together, but now he could get a look at her from head to toe.

Tia's curves were smooth and defined. There was just enough muscle on her to accentuate the slopes of her arms and legs, while also giving her a flat, trim torso. Her breasts were naturally large, however, and capped with erect, dark red nipples.

Clint's hands went to her breasts first, and Tia arched her back when she felt him massage her. She spread her legs for him and shifted just enough for Clint to get situated between them. He then moved his hands all the way down her sides until he was grasping her solid, rounded hips.

Allowing Clint to move her as he pleased, Tia leaned back and let out satisfied little moans as he worked his hands along her thighs. Those moans grew louder the instant his fingers drifted into the soft red hair between her legs.

As Clint crawled on top of her, he kept his hands on Tia's soft pussy. He rubbed her until the lips between her legs were wet and ready for him. By the time she reached down to stroke his penis, it was rigid and aching to be inside her.

Clint moved his hands up and sampled the enticing feel of her stomach. He could feel her squirming beneath him as every inch of her lower body struggled to get closer to him. When he started guiding himself into her, Tia reached down and gently eased herself open to accept him. She let out a trembling moan as he slid into her.

Using one hand to support himself, Clint massaged Tia's breasts with the other hand. All the while, he pumped his hips back and forth in a steady, powerful rhythm.

Tia rubbed one leg against the small of Clint's back while pushing her other foot against the wall of the wagon. The space might have been cramped and confined, but it felt warm and cozy once they let themselves forget about the rest of the world around them.

Biting down on her lower lip, Tia arched her back and began grinding her hips in quick circles. That sent chills through both of them and caused Clint to pump even more vigorously between her legs.

After speeding up his pace, Clint almost pulled out of her, waited, and then drove all the way inside her with one solid thrust. That caused Tia to pull in a deep, excited breath as her first orgasm washed over her. Clint could feel her heart pounding in her chest, and buried himself in her once more to take her to the limit.

Once she was able to see straight again, Tia gave Clint a bright smile and got him to roll over onto his side. She rolled right along with him, pulling the edges of the blankets up as she went to wrap both of them in their own little cocoon.

There was even less room to maneuver now, but that was just fine by Clint. After a little shifting, he was able to slip one arm over Tia's shoulders and one leg around her hips. She nestled right against him and squirmed until she was in just the right spot.

Clint was savoring the feel of Tia's breasts against his chest and the tickle of her hair against his skin. With those sensations still fresh, he felt a new one as the tip of his cock pressed against the wet lips of her pussy. She was the one to let out a breath as she took him inside her.

From this position, Clint fit tightly inside her. He pulled her close while pushing his hips forward until every inch of him was buried in her. From there, their bodies writhed under the blankets as he pumped in and out of her with a slow, insistent rhythm.

Tia closed her eyes and laid her head against Clint's

shoulder as he moved in and out of her. Clint wrapped her up in his arms and buried his face in the tangle of her thick, red hair. He could feel the muscles of her stomach tensing against him, which made it even more satisfying as he pumped into her again and again.

Soon, their breaths were coming in labored gasps and their arms were tightening around each other.

Tia's fingernails dug into Clint's back as she pressed her mouth against the blankets and let out a muffled groan.

Clint could feel his body responding to hers, bringing his own climax that much quicker. Rather than fight it, he let himself go and pumped into her with growing intensity.

Finally, Clint thrust one more time and exploded inside her. Tia arched her back and pulled him close until she climaxed as well. Their bodies trembled for a few moments before finally, she let him go.

"Now I see what you mean," Clint said breathlessly. "I feel like I could take on the whole world."

Tia let out another satisfied gasp and wiped the sweaty strands of hair from her face. "I feel like I need a nap."

FORTY-TWO

There were fights throughout the afternoon, but most of them were between the men who were working off debts to Hackett. A few of the professional fighters locked horns, but all of those bouts were more bluster than anything else.

Over the last few hours, Clint had spread the word about what was to happen among the fighters who'd been duped into spilling their blood in Mescall. Tia had done the same thing with the professional fighters, letting them all know what kind of man they were working for. Along the way, she got a good sense of who she could count on and who didn't mind tearing someone apart just so long as the price was right.

Once Clint and Tia had met up to compare what they'd learned, he gave the word and put the next phase of his plan into motion. It was the simplest part of the plan, actually, since it involved nothing at all.

When the time came for the last fight to be fought, everyone gathered in the pit, placed their bets, and looked down at the two men who were supposed to duke it out. Warren Nolen stood on one side of the pit while one of Tia's drinking buddies stood on the other.

The crowd whooped and hollered, building to a frenzy until Hackett stood up and shouted, "Fight!"

The fighters didn't move.

They didn't say a word or even raise their fists.

They did nothing.

"You heard me!" Hackett shouted. "I told you to fight!"

The crowd was getting anxious by now and started screaming down into the pit. "Fight! Fight! Fight! Fight!" they shouted until their voices started to get scratchy in their whiskey-ravaged throats.

Hackett jumped to his feet and rushed down to the edge of the pit. Reaching under his jacket, he drew the modified Colt that had been holstered there. "You men want a shot at this or any of that prize money, you'd best start swinging."

When he saw no reaction from either of the fighters, Hackett focused his seething eyes on Warren. "You want to see that whore sister of yours?" Hackett snarled. "Do your part right here and now, goddammit."

Either the crowd was losing interest or they were trying to make sense out of Hackett's growls. Either way, they quieted down just enough to make what came next echo through the pit like thunder over an open prairie.

"How about if I take a shot at that prize?" came a voice from the second row of seats carved out of soil and wood.

Every eye shifted to see Clint stand up and make his way to the edge of the pit. After a moment of stunned silence, the crowd erupted into such a wild state that it seemed they were about to tear the canvas roof right off of the main arena.

Hackett smiled and nodded, motioning for the crowd to quiet down. His guards had to step in and start throwing their weight around, but the noise eventually died to a more manageable level.

"You want to fight, Adams? You're more than welcome," Hackett said. "In fact, I'll even overlook the fact that you didn't make it through the previous rounds."

That was met with more applause as the crowd started chanting Clint's name.

"A-dams! A-dams! A-dams!"

Clint nodded and accepted the ovation. Finally, he raised his hands for quiet and got it less than two seconds later. He then let one of his hands fall to his side. The other slowly leveled off to point directly at the barrel-chested man standing perched on the edge of the pit.

"I'll fight for the prize," Clint said. "But only against you, Hackett. You're the man who took my property and I want you to hand it back."

"I'm not one of the fighters, Adams."

"Then just hand over what's rightfully mine and I'll be on my way. Otherwise, I'll have to come over there, take it from you, and show all these folks that you're nothing but a lot of talk hiding behind a lot of shotguns."

After being pushed around by Hackett's guards from the moment they walked into Mescall, there wasn't one man in that crowd who hadn't been thinking the exact words that Clint had just said out loud. Clint had seen that in every one of those drunken faces every time one of those guards had strutted by.

Not only did the crowd show its approval of the proposed fight, but it even started pushing back against the guards who were trying to calm it down. Men began challenging the guards directly until the guards inevitably started bringing up their shotguns.

"All right!" Hackett shouted. "No need for all the commotion. If this is the fight you want to see, this is the fight you'll get. It just might be a little unfair to the competitors who've already made it this far."

Even as Hackett spoke those words, the two fighters already in the pit were helping each other climb out. Warren looked over to Hackett and made a wide, sweeping gesture with his arm to welcome the barrel-chested man into the pit.

To Clint's surprise, Hackett not only agreed to the fight,

but seemed to be looking forward to it. When he looked across at Clint, Hackett smiled like a hungry wolf and started peeling off his jacket and shirt.

"It's been a little while since I've fought like this," Hackett said. "But I bet I've done it a whole lot more than you. Be sure to leave that pistol behind. You wouldn't want anyone to call you a cheat."

"Sure," Clint said as he unbuckled his gun belt and dropped it. "I just hope nobody makes off with that pistol while my back's turned."

"You heard the man," Hackett announced. "And if anyone else goes for their weapons, you'll be just as dead as Adams."

Pouncing on that opportunity to flex their muscles, the guards lifted their shotguns and took up their positions around the arena.

Clint jumped down into the pit and stripped off his shirt. Hackett was already prepared and was working out the kinks in his neck and shoulders.

Although Clint had a few years on Hackett, Hackett still had a build comparable to any of the other fighters. In fact, his torso was thick with muscle and covered in scars, marking him as a veteran of bare-knuckle brawling.

"This was a mistake, Adams," Hackett said as he looked up and nodded to Cal, who responded instantly to the signal. "But it's too late to back out now."

FORTY-THREE

Cal emerged from the tent after fighting his way through a crowd that was anxiously watching the opening punches get thrown. Once he was past the distracted drunks, Cal bolted into the relative calm that had enveloped the rest of Mescall.

"You two," Cal said to the pair of guards at the front entrance of the tent. "Come with me."

"What's going on in there?"

"Never mind that. We need to round up that blonde and the rest of those women and children."

"All of them? What for?"

"Mr. Hackett wants to make sure he gets good use from his bargaining chips," Cal said. "Some of the fighters in there need to be reminded what they're fighting for."

Shrugging, the two guards followed Cal through the camp's makeshift streets. The path in between the tents was more crooked than a snake's backbone and took them into the same part of Mescall where Hackett's personal wagon was parked.

Cal headed straight for another wagon that was just as solid as Hackett's. The main difference with this one was that the small windows on the sides of the wagon had been boarded shut. Digging a key from his pocket, Cal reached out for the door at the back of the wagon and unlocked it. He pulled it open and stuck the business end of his shotgun inside.

"All of you get out of there," Cal barked. "Make one wrong move and we'll blow your fucking heads off."

After Cal had backed away a few steps, a row of frightened people came out of the wagon. Most of them were women with blackened eyes, blood on their lips, and rips in their clothes. Katrina Nolen was among them, and she stepped out just ahead of another woman who had two young boys clinging to her skirts.

The kids couldn't have been more than five or six years old and were the only ones in Mescall who were even more frightened than the women piling out of that wagon. Counting those two children, there were eight prisoners in all. Apart from the minor bumps and cuts they had, it was obvious that they hadn't had a wink of sleep in some time.

"Come along with us," Cal said. "We're gonna convince your men to do what they're told. Otherwise you're all gonna die together."

Neither of the other two guards took a step after Cal had started to walk. They were looking around with confusion spreading across their faces.

"Shouldn't there be some other men posted here?"

Just as those words escaped the guard's mouth, a wooden pole sliced through the air and connected squarely against his head. He staggered back without knowing where the impact had come from and before he could figure it out, a second blow connected with his temple.

Cal swung his shotgun in the direction of the movement he saw, but most of his view was blocked by the neighboring wagon. All he'd seen was the blur of the wooden pole going through the air. He fired his shotgun in that direction, but merely took a sizable chunk out of the other wagon.

The footsteps came from every direction. They rushed

in like a tidal wave to surround Cal and the other remaining guard. That second guard pulled his trigger, but only after his hand had been crushed by another wooden pole grasped in the hands of one of Hackett's reluctant fighters.

Trying to look in every direction at once, Cal saw several of the fighters supposedly under Hackett's thumb now beating the other guards with broken pieces of wood clutched in desperate hands. The shotgun had been wrenched out of Cal's grasp and had already been turned on one of the other guards, forcing that man to drop his weapon.

Rather than be overpowered by a bunch of amateur fighters, Cal made a grab for the pistol hanging at his side. Just as he was about to clear leather, he heard the distinctive *click-click* of two hammers being pulled back into firing position.

"Not a good idea, friend," Rick Hartman said from behind a shotgun similar to the one Cal had been holding. "I may not be as good a shot as the man I took this from, but I don't really need to be very good to hit any of you at this distance."

"You stupid son of a bitch," Cal said, making sure to keep his hands from moving. "Do you really think you can get away with this? How far do you think you'll get?"

"Who's going to stop us?" Hartman asked. "You?" Nodding back to a spot behind him, he added, "Or them?"

Cal took a look for himself and saw the other guards who'd been watching over the prisoners. All four of those men were piled up like so much firewood. They'd been beaten up and tied with ragged strips of canvas.

It didn't take long for Cal to see where the canvas had come from. The rows of tents just beyond the wagons had all been pulled down and torn apart. The covering had been shredded to use as rope and the poles had been snapped apart and used as weapons. According to the lumps on all the guards' heads, those poles were very effective weapons, indeed.

When Cal looked back at Rick Hartman, the fear in his eyes was plain for everyone to see.

"I think this is the last go-around for Mescall," Hartman said.

One of the guards was putting up a bit of a fight, but none of the men he was swinging at were backing down. On the contrary, they looked at the guard without a hint of fear, took a few punches, and then delivered plenty more of their own.

Hartman shook his head and kept the shotgun pointed at the guards while the rest of the fighters bound their arms and legs with shredded strips of canvas. "The next time you boys decide to take prisoners, you might not want to make them into fighters. As you can see, that tends to backfire."

Struggling to keep his chin up, Cal said, "There's plenty more of us."

Hartman nodded. "I know. But there's a whole lot more of us. And the ones that haven't already gotten away to bring back the law are dealing with your boss right now."

"Hackett and the others will tear you apart. Gunsmith or not."

"We'll just see about that," Hartman replied with confidence.

FORTY-FOUR

The fist slammed against its intended jaw with staggering power. It had come at the end of a flurry of blows and had all of the weight of its owner behind it. Considering that the owner was Dale Hackett, that was a considerable amount of weight.

Clint took the hit as best he could, despite the fact that his eyesight turned blurry and fractured for a moment. Even through the fog behind his eyes, however, he could see the grin on Hackett's face.

"Had enough yet, Adams?" Hackett asked. "Or do I need to put you down for good?"

Clint's response was a punch aimed at Hackett's belly. When the other man went to block, Clint lashed out with his other fist aimed a few feet higher. Hackett didn't fall for the attempt to fake him out. He let the first shot bounce against his solid gut and swatted the second away with his beefy forearm.

"I think you have had enough!" Hackett announced. He played up to the crowd with waving hands and a strut around a section of the pit.

Clint started to get up and took a swing at Hackett's ribs. His arm was slowed by the last several shots he'd taken and was immediately caught under Hackett's arm. Before Clint could take another swing, he felt his other arm become trapped as well.

Hackett stood toe-to-toe with Clint, smiling directly into his face. "You could'a done this the easy way, Adams," he said so only Clint could hear. "But instead, you chose to bleed. I hope you realize that I can't let you leave this pit." Snapping his head forward, Hackett pounded his forehead into the top of Clint's nose. "I'll just have to bury you here."

Struggling against Hackett's ironlike bear hug, Clint soon realized there was no way for him to escape the hold. He stomped his feet and kicked Hackett's shins, but the other man might as well have been made from stone and barely winced at each blow.

Hackett's arms cinched in tighter and tighter, squeezing the air right out of Clint's lungs. Clint felt his ribs bending inward, and knew they were about to start snapping like dry twigs. He looked up to the top of the arena and saw a familiar face stepping into the tent.

Rick Hartman gave Clint a quick nod and waved frantically. Behind Hartman, the men who'd been tricked into becoming fighters started streaming into the tent. Their women and children were coming right along with them.

Clint sucked in a breath and leaned to one side. Using all the strength he could muster, he pulled one arm free and used it to deliver a straight shot right into Hackett's chin. The move had been so quick that Hackett didn't even know he'd let Clint's arm slip free until the heel of that hand was driving into his face.

The shot didn't do much damage, but it stunned Hackett enough for him to let up on some of the pressure he'd been applying to Clint's ribs. He felt Clint kick him again, only this time there was a whole new fire in Clint's blows.

Now, Clint was the one to lean back and snap his head forward. One advantage to having taken the punishment he had before was that he didn't feel much of the pain from the head butt he'd just delivered. In the next moment, Clint was able to pull in a full breath and Hackett was staggering away from him.

Reaching up to dab at the blood trickling down his face, Hackett asked, "Got yer second wind, huh?"

"This is all over, Hackett."

"What do you mean?"

"The fight and your whole business. It's all over." He shifted his eyes up into the crowd and got Hackett to do the same.

The first thing Hackett noticed was the significant drop in the number of his guards. What men he did see were no longer holding shotguns. Instead, they were being held at gunpoint by a group of very angry men who no longer had a reason to do as they were told.

That left the few guards who'd been on the edge of the pit right alongside Hackett when his fight with Clint had started. Those three guards looked around with desperation and found that their support was fading fast.

"Well, don't just stand there, you idiots!" Hackett shouted. "Use those shotguns!"

Hearing that caused the rest of the crowd to jump from where they were sitting and bolt for the door. As much as they liked watching fights, they didn't have much of a desire to be in one. The prospect of being in the same room with those guards once Hackett had given the order to fire was even less appealing.

The arena was cleared in a matter of moments.

The next wave of bodies to come through the entrance were the few straggling guards who'd been elsewhere in the camp until now. They charged in, saw what was going on, and immediately readied their weapons. Before they could fire a shot, the professional fighters descended upon them, making quick work of the surprised gunmen. Tia was in the thick of that fight and soon had a shotgun of her own.

One of the guards at the edge of the pit raised his shotgun to fire at Clint. A fraction of a second before the blast sounded, Clint rolled backward and out of the line of fire. Although the lead punched a hole in the floor of the pit, Clint had knocked against the wall and had nowhere else to go.

The guards at the edge of the pit smiled now that Clint was backed against the wall. They brought their shotguns to their shoulders, ignoring the rest of the chaos going on around them.

Clint straightened up and reached both hands straight over his head.

"Too late to surrender now, Adams," Hackett snarled. "You just cost me a fortune, so I'll take yer life in trade. Ready boys?"

Before Hackett gave the order to fire, Clint hopped up and reached just a little higher over his head. One hand found the gun that he'd dropped before entering the pit and he pulled that gun from its holster to fill his fist.

Clint's arm snapped to eye level. From there, he pointed at each shotgunner in turn and pulled his trigger in quick succession. Each of the guards reeled back as hot lead drilled through their foreheads. One by one, the guards dropped, leaving Hackett all by himself inside the pit.

"I'll be damned," Hackett grunted as he slowly lifted his hands in surrender.

"You sure will," came a voice from a few rows up.

Warren Nolen stepped down to the edge of the pit, sighting along the barrel of the gun he'd taken from one of the guards.

Shifting his aim to cover Hackett, Clint said, "Don't, Warren. This is all over. The law's on their way and Hackett will get what's coming to him."

"He's got to pay, Clint."

"And he will. Just let it happen the right way."

Letting out a breath, Warren lowered his gun. Rick Hartman was right there to take it from him.

"That's the last of the guards," Hartman said as he dropped down to stand next to Clint. Studying Clint's battered face, he leaned over and whispered, "You sure went all out to keep Hackett busy. Did he get in a few lucky punches?"

"Lucky, my ass," Clint replied. "The man knows how to fight. Good thing, too," he added when he saw the smug grin on Hackett's face. "Because he'll need to be able to handle himself when he gets tossed into a Texas jailhouse."

"And he won't have long to wait," Hartman said. "The first men rode out of here this morning and should be back with some deputies any moment."

"That just leaves one loose end," Clint said.

Tia waved down from where she'd been rounding up Hackett's guards and said, "You must be talking about this." She tossed Clint's modified Colt through the air.

The pistol felt at home in Clint's hand. Now that the familiar weight of iron and lead was right where it should be, all was right in Clint's world. "Thanks," he said to Tia.

The redhead winked and turned toward another guard who was starting to put up a fight. She eagerly joined her friends in making that guard regret his decision.

"Actually," Hartman said, "that's not the only loose end."

FORTY-FIVE

The poker table was almost full.

The men in the saloon had been playing for a few hours, which was enough for them to form a loose friendship that came along with small stakes. Their table was set up in the back of a quiet saloon in Austin. After pitching their antes into the middle, one of the men dealt the next hand and started in on the next round of small talk.

"Say, you boys hear about that trouble out west? The law from three different towns rounded up a bunch of kidnappers and thieves."

"Really?" asked the first man to bet. "I hear it was fights they held for money. Too many men died in those things. I say good riddance." He looked over to the next man in line and asked, "What do you think about that nonsense?"

The next man shrugged and tossed in his coins. "Ehhhh, I try not to get involved in that sort of thing. At least, ehh-hhh, not anymore."

Watch for

GUNMAN'S CROSSING

291st novel in the exciting GUNSMITH series
from Jove

Coming in March!

GIANT ACTION! GIANT ADVENTURE!

THE GUNSMITH

GIANT

GIANT WESTERNS FEATURING THE GUNSMITH

THE GHOST OF BILLY THE KID
0-515-13622-0

LITTLE SURESHOT AND THE WILD WEST SHOW
0-515-13851-7

DEAD WEIGHT
0-515-14028-7

AVAILABLE WHEREVER BOOKS ARE SOLD OR AT PENGUIN.COM

J799

J. R. ROBERTS
THE GUNSMITH

GIANT-SIZED ADVENTURE FROM AVENGING ANGEL LONGARM.

LONGARM AND THE DEADLY DEAD MAN
0-515-13547-X

LONGARM AND THE BARTERED BRIDES
0-515-13834-7